FATHER, FORGIVE THEM

By
John Becker, S.J.

This book is a work of fiction. Places, events, and
situations in this story are purely fictional. Any
resemblance to actual persons, living or dead, is
coincidental.

ISBN: 1-4033-8887-3 (e-book)
ISBN: 1-4033-8888-1 (Paperback)

Library of Congress Control Number: 2002095396

This book is printed on acid free paper.

Printed in the United States of America
Bloomington, IN

1stBooks - rev. 08/09/2007

Acknowledgements

AMDG

Father, Forgive Them would never have seen the light of day without the patient help of many friends. I am very grateful to each of them.

ONE

"Well, what do you think of that, Father?" There was the slightest emphasis on the *think*—surprisingly, rather than the *that*. Not grossly so, but laced with just a tiny trickle of truculence.

What he thought of it was pretty pedestrian: *Your son—well, stepson—is just plain lazy. And he would cheat his way through every exam if I didn't move him away from everybody else the first time he glances at his neighbor's paper.* But he couldn't say that. Or could he? In a tactful way so that the father could understand and not go ballistic (how are you supposed to make sense of that metaphor?—even if you *know* what it means).

"Dr. Brandt, your son has failed all of the book tests this semester. There were three so far. Each of these was a major assignment."

It was early Sunday evening. An insouciant mockingbird was having fun outside the open window—telling the world why it's wrong to kill him—as if he had read Harper Lee's novel. And the March sun was still cool enough to make the garden outside the old-fashioned twelve-paned windows glow quietly, each with a life of its own. He had come to his classroom after supper to correct a class or two of *Hamlet* essays. Somehow he had to escape for a little while all of the other things that needed doing and stalked him in his Jesuit residence room—that curriculum report, the letter that would be long to his cousin about the Church's stand on birth control, the list of "books that must be read" former student Harry

1

Kohler had requested for his son. But talking to the parents was important. If very distracting.

Father Wolfe found his classroom a pleasant place to work. In the oldest part of the school—part of the original 1928 structure—it was old-fashioned—with a 20-foot high ceiling and sash-balanced windows. And through those windows in his classroom he could see the kindly statue of the Sacred Heart that had been blessing the pond around Him and the green berm-accoutred lawn that introduced the passing motorists on Kennedy to the school and campus—now much enlarged with a gym and tennis courts and football and baseball fields—that George Wheatley had built for the Jesuits just before the big crash. He had been a stiff and pompous—to judge by his picture on the wall just outside the principal's office—but wise and lucky investor: he had brought grapes to the Valley, and their wine had made him ridiculously wealthy. He had idolized his wife Helen and wanted a fitting memorial to her. And on seventeen acres at what had then been the edge of the city he had built this now old two-story classroom building and the chapel behind the Jesus statue and the residence for the Jesuit Fathers and offices on the southern vertical leg of that architectural H that had its feet to the west.

Wisely the architects had come up with grace that spelled the kind of peace that Academe demanded.

And Father Wolfe had fitted this classroom with enough memories, enough memorabilia, to mimic a lifetime. On a waist-high shelf all around the room were more or less up-to-date computers, the tools he was using to train the students to write quickly and accurately and deeply in an electronics age. Model airplanes hung from the ceiling. Sailing ships models garnished every open wall space around the room. There was George Halbert's Eight Ball he had sent when he become editor in chief of that prestigious magazine. It was a regulation pool eight-ball, black with the white circle around the *8*, set on what looked like a miniature volcano in a tray the size of a coffee cup saucer, all jet black.

There was a grey-white, foot-long model of an old Boeing F4B4 Navy pre-World War II fighter. Hayden Berg had offered this brightly detailed echo as a not-so-veiled bribe just before final exams fifteen, no, sixteen years ago—well aware that Father Wolfe had commented during one class that that venerable aircraft was the loveliest airplane ever created.

Across the wall opposite the door and over the windows in four-inch-high Times New Roman type was "Our Business Is Heir Conditioning." Alex Krause had computer-fashioned that one after Father Wolfe had used it as an example of a pun—one of the many figures of speech employed by the great writers in their agony to express the reality that belied the simple word. And then it became the perfect example of how to capitalize a title—everything except interior conjunctions and articles and prepositions. Father Luke smiled to himself at how his whole life had become interwebbed with the vagaries of the English language.

And there were several mobiles. One of Bugs Bunny characters. Another of famous authors, their portraits set in cameo-like frames.

The walls of the classroom were painted a bright and deep yellow, Father Wolfe's favorite color. With the help of several students he had done that painting

3

himself the summer before. And when they had finished, current senior Larry Curtland—who had had him as a sophomore teacher—had gone out to buy the eight-inch-high wooden letters *AMDG*. He had then painted them tomato red—befitting at least one of the Kino school colors of red and white, and, when they were dry, had tacked them high on the front wall. Everyone in the school—even the newest freshman— knew those letters were the epitome of everything the founder of the Jesuits—St. Ignatius Loyola—stood for: Ad Majorem Dei Gloriam, For the Greater Glory of God. Above it, Gary Blaettler had insisted they hang the two-and-a-half-foot Oberammergau-carved crucifix he had brought back from his Europe trip with Father Gorski and twenty-two fellow Kino students. It was no ordinary crucifix: although the naked body of Christ— only a scrap of rag hung across His waist—was in such agony that it seemed he would wrench Himself off the cross, a quiet smile floating across His lips.

And there was the talking frog by the door that Jimmy Jagozinski had brought in one windy January day. Jimmy had primed the tape to say, "And where do you think you are going, young man?" in a bloated stentorian W.C. Fields voice, perfectly enunciated and demanding. And Jimmy's classmates had insisted that it sit on the shelf by the door that was in the middle of the east wall, opposite the windows—to be activated by anyone carelessly gesturing as he turned the lights on or off.

There was the five-foot-tall poster of the Sistine Chapel's *Last Judgment* that Billy Eckleman had brought back from his Europe trip; it was a great prop for discussion about much of the literature—heaven, hell, Jesus' judgment, Mary's intercession. Phil—what was his last name? He could see in his mind's eye his boxy jaw and his wire-brush haircut—Latham had sent him that Mexican Flag from Guadalajara—that must have been in 1959—that now festooned the seven feet above the doorway.

So many students.

A jet growled overhead. The mockingbird upped the ante.

"He has written none of the assigned essays. There were six of those—we're talking only about this second semester. He gets involved in class discussion only when challenged, and then has little to say—although what he does say then usually fails to hide his deep and probing intelligence. Do you understand that for all practical purposes he has done nothing to show his abilities in this course? So that when you tell me he has won the $2000 K Award for the best essay on the nutritional advantages of"—Fr. Wolfe paused slightly to emphasize the alliteration—"Kordoff Koffee Krunch, I congratulate him—and you. But that really has nothing to do with the matter at hand." Did he sound angry? Sarcastic? Impatient? He hoped not.

There was only breathing in the receiver. Stertorous—surprising from someone with such a cosmopolitan voice. "So you're saying he can't graduate." The anger underneath the comment threatened eruption. The mockingbird in full bright voice suddenly and sharply flouted Doctor Brandt's unhappiness. C below the scale to G on the staff. Fee-ee-ee.

Father Luke paused to listen to the bird's two up two down that followed. Then a trill that found nothing but joy in the whole wide world. The sun had just dipped over the edge slowly. To wherever it went at night.

"He can graduate if he makes *some* effort to do the work of the semester. You're a doctor. You can understand quid pro quo. You bring diagnosis and—"

Father Wolfe put the phone gently back in the cradle. The line had gone dead. Greg will never do any of that work. And his new father cannot understand that he just doesn't care about anything academic.

He stared at the pack of papers in front of him. *Hamlet would never have made it in today's business world. He was too wishy-washy. He always hadda* (he green-circled the solecism) *prove every step he took. He couldn't just skewer his—*

Father Wolfe stood up, walked to the classroom door and straightened the frog. Someone had bumped it askew from its forward position of greeting.

What *could* he do to light a fire under Greg Farrell? He was back at his desk again, looking out beyond the jacaranda tree at the white Jesus statue. As a teacher he had tried every sleight of hand in his bag of tricks. He had been gently sarcastic in class. He had laughed at Greg's phony excuses. He had given it to him man to man, straight from the shoulder. He had urged the boy's friends to lean on him. Was it his failure as an English teacher? As a priest? As a man? He had been on and off haunted by the Bill O'Malley *America* magazine article he had read years ago. Its point was brutally skinny: teachers are salesmen: if nobody buys, they are failures. And so his seemingly somnambulant students never ceased to jostle his pedagogic conscience. Just like a doctor: no cures, no more patients. Patience.

TWO

"Hiya, Father Luke. Correct my paper yet?" Lighthearted. Buoyant. Slightly mocking. But straight from the shoulder. Like a Marine.

Fr. Luke looked up. He had finished correcting only three papers. In the doorway to the classroom— twenty-five feet from his desk—stood Tony Santos. Tall—six feet two of him, at least. He had his arm around the waist of a diminutive girl with a Barbie Doll-perfect face and a Barbra Streisand nose and very black lustrous hair cut in what looked like a 1920's bob to Father Luke's old-fashioned eyes and parted on her left side. Tony was pulling her to himself as though she could not stand alone. She wriggled just slightly in response. Slightly backlit from the hall florescents, their faces dark, with coronas around his shaved head and her black hair.

"Father," the couple was in the classroom now, "I want you to meet Alice Grunch." They all laughed. The mockingbird outside did a bright contrapuntal adagio.

So much for a quiet evening of correcting papers— although it was always great fun to chat with his students. "How did you two get in here? I thought the place was tomb-sealed."

"Mall door was open, Father. Bunch of teachers in the teachers' lounge. What're they doing here on a Sunday night? They must've left it open." He could see the couple clearly now that they were fifteen feet away. Tony Santos. What had been curly black hair was now closely shaved. *Why do the kids do that? In football season I can understand the urge to simplify.*

8

But why look like a billiard ball the rest of the year? Sharp nose borrowed from an El Greco Saint. Dark complexion darkened by his three-day five-o'clock shadow on his lean Philip II face. How did he manage to evade the Dean's cold stare and cold-water razor? And the girl with raven—that's the way the old poets would have described it—hair and alabaster skin. He wondered if you really could see through it.

"Is that, umm, really her name, Ton?"

"Your class examples always include Alice Grunch, Father. And so I thought— Actually it's Rita Poulos. She's Greek. I mean her parents are from Greece. She's from Michigan. Grand Rapids. They moved here last October."

Father smiled. His hand absentmindedly went up to straighten the few strands of white hair that vied with one another to cover his otherwise bald head. This was the reticent Tony who never raised his hand in class. Who had to have answers pried out of him. With question after question. *If only I could get Rita into the classroom when it's time for him to recite!*

"*Tikanis.*"

In a moment he was back in the parking lot of the Star Theater in the San Francisco Mission district. His first job. Directing movie-goers to the empty parking slots. Bouncing mis-positioned cars that straddled two parking places back where they belonged. Occasionally valet-ing a Packard. Or a Lincoln.

There he had met Alessandro—Alex who spent a good part of the day chopping onions at the open back door of his father's greasy spoon that opened on the east side of the parking lot.

9

Two years older than Luke's sixteen, he had explained that he attended Greek school every day after his regular school, and had done that every day since first grade.

And *tikanis*, Alex—he had a way of looking up from under the onion business at hand in a way that bespoke the wisdom of the ages—said, meant *hello*. And you answered with *Eemay kala. Gaybose eesay essee*. Well, that was the way he had heard it. And what he had memorized—and more vividly than the classical Greek he had tried to learn in class a few years later.

"Oh, I don't speak Greek, Father." Rita looked out at him from under her long black lashes and smiled—mostly with her eyes—her mother-always-taught-us-to-be-nice-to-strangers smile. She had a little-girl politeness about her. Airy. Simple. Unaffected. Yet somehow completely full of life. And verve. And excitement. Like a grown-up playful kitten.

"Neither do I. But I like to show off with the word or two I—um—don't know." Father Luke gave them his caught-with-his-hand-in-the-cookie-jar smile.

"Then you must be Scots." It was clear she liked to be teased. "To judge by your dress."

"Jumper, Father. No, but Cathy Ogilvie gave it to me. She said it was her family plaid, and I love its quiet blue pattern. So much prettier than our Campbell-blue plaid skirts we must wear at Mother Teresa." She did a little girl curtsy, and smiled. It *was* a quiet blue. With a fresh white blouse under it. And it somehow fitted her quiet and unaffected freshness. And long enough to be modest by anybody's standards and short enough to avoid shouting that she of all womankind was a good girl.

"We demonstrated outside the Best Way abortion clinic on Sixteenth last Saturday, Father." Tony wasn't getting jealous just because she was talking to the old priest, was he? No. Tony smiled. *Beamed* was the word the old novelists used. This girl certainly brought out the best in Tony. "Rita belongs to the Pro-Life Club at Mother Teresa's. Like, that's where she goes to school." He gestured vaguely toward the Catholic girls' school a quarter mile to the east. "And she asked me to go with her. What could I say?"

Why is he telling me that?

"You oughta sponsor a club like that here, Father.

There it is, the answer.

"Will you sponsor us if we start it? After all, you tell us how horrible abortion is every chance you get in class."

"I do?"

"C'mon, Father. I'll just have to start taping you."

A smile and a wave and they were gone.

What a wonderful gift You give us in love—especially young love—the tenderness the boy feels often for the first time in his life for the strength the girl offers.

Jesus, give these two kids the gift of falling in love with each other, simply and entirely. Not just in the pleasure the other person gives, but each other, the person—so that together they can chastely serve You in the cleanness and innocence of abstinence before marriage and after the big I Do in a whole houseful of joy-filled and -giving children. Like what I once wanted. For me. And for Janey.

THREE

Had he been that fond of Janey? His mind synapsed back to his school days. How do you compare total absorption in another human being?

With Tony and Rita gone, the room had turned lonely, and he was suddenly caught up in the memory. His mind refused to accost the *Hamlet* papers.

He had gone through the whole of St. Augustine's Grammar School there at Fortieth Avenue and Rembrandt right smack in the middle of San Francisco's Sunset District. He and Janey had both been in the same classrooms together for eight years. But he had scarcely been aware of her for the books and the desks and Sister Petronilla and all the other Sisters with their selfless concern for him (he found it difficult to reconcile derogatory comments about nuns by graduates of Catholic schools with the good and kind and gentle women who had coaxed him through those formative years) and their often improbable names.

But he had met Janet Peer quite accidentally at a mixer sponsored for the incoming freshmen at St. Luke's. And he had suddenly noticed her. Funny, he would have trouble describing her today. She was rather blonde, he remembered, but not startlingly so. And her hair, close to her head and rather short, had a bit of a curl. Was it natural? Probably: it wasn't like her to be phony in anything. She had a pert nose and very small ears. What color eyes? Bright blue, yes, they had been—were still?—blue, weren't they? There was a robust vitality to her: she loved the sports she excelled in—volleyball and tennis. And she was good, at least in tennis. His memory was still bright and sharp of her leap into the air, tiny white skirt snapping and floating over her brown legs, her eyes concentrating totally on the ball as she smashed it yards beyond his wild scramble to cover and return it—that his bad leg kept him from getting it was no more than a male chauvinist's unrealistic excuse.

But the attraction had been something deeper, somehow. Janet—but she preferred to be called Janey for a reason he never did find out—Peer was somehow good. And true and just right. Through and through. You could talk to her without suddenly wondering if your left ear was missing or your nose was on straight. And he didn't have the slightest suspicion of what she was getting him into.

Was it that same sort of simplicity in Rita that had bubbled up this memory of so long ago as though it were yesterday? What was it, sixty—sixty-five years? Long enough.

It had not been until the latter part of his high school junior year that he had started dating her. Regularly and often. His very ordinary grades had slalomed down to rub elbows with those of members on the academic probation list. Still, as often as not, they had borrowed her brother Joe's black Deucey (the throwaway name in every young male's lexicon for a 1932 Ford) usually with Bobby Thurston and his Cathy—Catherine Unger (the class wag had suggested that with a pairing of patronymics like that they could make a mint in the restaurant business)—in the rumble seat—to find a high school or parish or club social where they could dance away the evening. Big Bands

13

and Swing were in. The Dorsey Brothers. Glenn Miller.

She was so good, so holy, it was almost with reluctance that he touched her—even to hold her while they danced. And even then, often enough, she would slip out of his arms to do her own pas de deux with flashing eyes and big swinging skirt and arms out wide and fingers snapping to the beat.

Then suddenly and vividly the day was with him when roly-poly Brother Gerard called him into the principal's office. The kids called him Brother Sausage—behind his back: somehow he could never find a cassock large enough so that he didn't look as though he were about to be squeezed out of it. This was St. Luke's High School down in the Mission District, and Luke Wolfe had gone there partly because it was his namesake and partly because he somehow detested the Jesuit school in what had been an old bakery on the Hilltop next to their University. Why he had felt that antipathy he could never conjure up.

"Luke, you're a big boy now. And you have to take the responsibility for yourself." Brother Gerard had pulled out a large red handkerchief and rubbed his nose, blew it—noisily—and then looked Luke in the eye. "You have to do *some* work in each of your classes or you cannot graduate. I know, I know, the war's just about over and such a trivial matter does not matter." He smiled, probably at the redundancy. "Don't your parents care?"

"Of course."

"Well." He looked down at the file open to Luke's first-quarter report card.

"But they figure it's me and my life and what I want to do with it. They're very disappointed. But they're not on my back." Had he really said that? Or had he fitted a later cliché into the memory?

And his teachers made sarcastic remarks. Or flat-out told him what he ought to do.

But he continued to spend as much of his free time with Janey as he could. If it wasn't worship, it was something doing a great job as a stand in.

The insomniac mockingbird outside brought him back to the classroom. It was velvet black outside the window—Phoenix's gift of kindly night, the time to shed the chrysalis of day for the butterfly of sleep—or was it the other way around?

And he found himself praying the same prayer again. *Lord Jesus, bring these two kids to really love one another—not just in the pleasure and exhilaration of being in love—so that they can keep their love sacred to give to one another when they shout to the whole world "for richer, for poorer, in sickness and in health, forever."*

Eleven o'clock? The clock on the back wall—George Hannah's contribution—caroled out the bright warning of a Cardinal. Luke closed the cover on the folder. Still fifteen more to check. As he stood up, he stifled the groan—so many movements hurt, hips, legs, shoulder—he daily promised himself he would never admit to publicly, short-stepped it to the door, turned off the light. "And where do you think you're going, young man?" the frog croaked. It was loud and bright and sharp in the surrounding dark silence. And the tone neatly mimicked his own when he made sardonic comments to the class. He closed the door and locked

15

it and started to shuffle down the hall toward the middle corridor. Then, with a thought, he lengthened his stride and strode on with a farmer's stretched gait to the Jesuit residence on the other side of the chapel, fifty yards to the south.

Pain or no pain, you can't give in.

In five minutes he was asleep in his bed in his room.

FOUR

"For God's sake, Father—um, this is Lieutenant William Higgins—get down here as soon as you can."

Well, it certainly *was* for God's sake: at 2:23 in the morning he wasn't going to rush down to wherever *here* was for any other reason.

"Where is *here*, Bill?" As soon as his bedside phone brought him the deep and sonorous voice with the sandpaper edge, he had been instantly returned to the classroom of twenty years ago. Billy Higgins had sat in the second row from the door, fourth seat back. And now he was Lieutenant William Higgins. The voice hadn't changed. The insistent, leaning-forward, you-aren't-listening-to-me syllables were still the same.

"Jordan Street County Jail—Jordan Boulevard and Third Avenue, southwest corner."

"It can't wait till morning, Bill?"

"It *is* morning, Father, and I'm going crazy. We're all going crazy down here. This kid that says he used to be your friend—Larry Curtland—keeps confessing in a voice that keeps us all awake. He says he killed his father." And in his mind's ear Luke could hear Larry Curtland's small slit mouth under those bright, beady eyes saying "I killed my father."

"Did he?"

"Father, come down and give us a handle on this."

Used to be his friend.

Clothes. He dressed economically but without hurry. When he hurried he forgot things. Priest clothes—they wanted a priest. Black shirt. Funny white square-box plastic collar. Black pants. He gave

17

the Norelco a chance to do its thing, briefly. Ran the comb through the few white strands. He jammed the Green Bay Packers cap on top and brought them to disarray again.

Quiet. Be quiet in closing the door. Don't want to wake any of the brethren.

The Jesuit residence that was attached to the south end of the student chapel, opposite the school classroom building on the north end of the chapel, was all of a piece in its relaxed California Mission adobe style. Pseudo-adobe was a better way to describe it, perhaps, more like the old Franciscan missionaries would have liked to have built if they had had modern portland cement and rebars and enormous cranes and clear glass.

He tiptoed down the second-floor hall. Past Al's room. And Pierre's.

How much longer would he be passing Pierre's door and its "Growing Old Ain't For Sissies" bumpersticker tacked under his name? Father Pierre— his mother never really learned to speak English, and as a result her children's names and much of the rest of her life was Gallic—Atkins had been a student at Kino in its very earliest days, had returned as a young Jesuit in training and then, after ordination, to first teach chemistry—until his hands fought back at the chemicals with skin lesions—and then had become the President of the whole operation, the Rector of the Jesuit community and the Principal of the 500-student school all rolled into one. And he had thrived as the school had prospered under his gentle personality that aggressively scrambled for excellence—God's precision in mathematical formulae, the logic and poetry of words and moral conclusions, the reverent offering to the students of Jesus as their role model, mentor and friend for life. That, even when no one really knew how the next bill would be paid. And now he was pushing ninety, paper thin, but alive with a bright-eyed sense of humor that could still set the whole table on a roar—more in the way of Bob Hope than Jay Leno, of course. Would his next bout with the flu blow him away?

Well, at least there would be no trouble finding a community car free at this time of night. In the dim light under the dusty bulb, he took Number Five keys and signed his name. Till when? He scribbled *five ayem*. Without bothering much to make it legible.

It took exactly 14-1/2 minutes to pull into one of the jail parking slots. Straight down Kennedy past the Elizabethan Apartments where the old Carnation Creamery lived five years before, past the robust but not quite stately Imerdo box, the aloof Southero Bank Building with its million fly-eyes window-walls conjured up in an architectural nightmare out of a horror movie peering down on the mere humans below with supercilious irony. In the half light it seemed to be an Egyptian phallic megalith raised to the memory of the man who made it and the money he worshiped. And finally the frail, old, sad Lafayette Hotel with the hundred-foot antenna tower and blinking red light on its head.

The Maricopa County Jail was a new building. Unexpectedly tender, motherly on the outside. Like a new-baked loaf of whole wheat bread. North to south. Two stories, with a basement below. Less than a year old. But already it looked used, abused. Desert dust-brown. He pushed open the rather dirty door, climbed the four steps and asked for Lieutenant Higgins.

Only to find he was talking to the lieutenant himself. Foolish. He felt foolish. Like the day in class—ten, twelve years ago. It was a freshman class, and they were taking *Romeo and Juliet* apart. When they got to the end of Old Capulet's lamenting what he thought was the death of the daughter he had bullied to marry the wrong man, bright-eyed William Higgins had politely asked if the over-enthusiastic response, laced with apt metaphors like "Death lies on her like an untimely frost / On the fairest flower of the field" didn't adroitly illustrate Gertrude's "[T]he lady doth protest too much" in *Hamlet*. Of course it did. But what was a freshman doing coming up with such an apt and such a mature comment, particularly with regard to Shakespeare, the bane of high school males? After that startling comment, he, Father Wolfe, had been so taken by surprise that he had been able to delve out of his memory simply nothing to say to comment on Billy's words. Save "Yes, of course." Foolish.

Lieutenant Higgins was already there at the desk, standing behind the receptionist's empty chair. Looking picture-perfect—the defender of law and order and abused women and little kids. The man we all knew would take care of us if we were threatened. And now looking as fresh as though it were only nine o'clock in the morning. "Father." It was fact. And conclusion. Still pushy. And somehow a sigh. "Come on down to his cell." His voice still had its scratchy edge. "We can put you two in a lawyer room."

What's this all about? It was a natural question. But Luke said nothing.

As they passed the steel lacing of the cells, prisoners were standing and hanging on the bars and trying to peer down the gangway. It looked to be a hundred yards long, a little too far to throw a football. Ten feet wide. The only color was on the ceiling—a surprisingly stagnant green. One overhead fluorescent lightbox flickered in its embarrassed attempt to join its neighbors' insistence on lighting the remotest corner.

From what sounded like miles back in the cage they were passing, a voice floated eerily. "What the hell is going on?" It was a quavering sing-song, cigarette-frazzled voice, but belligerent. "People been walking up and down all night. And tell that guy to clam up. We wanna sleep."

Somebody *was* talking in a very loud voice from the end of the corridor. It was impossible to make out the words. And then they were there.

"Well, Larry." It was almost as though there was no steel door between them. Lieutenant Higgins and Father Wolfe had reached the end of the corridor, the last cage.

And the two words had popped out of the priest's mouth as soon as he saw the boy. The boy he saw before him looked like Larry Curtland, but he didn't at all seem to *be* the Larry Curtland of this past school year. The vital always-ready-to-tease boy was gone. A tough, serious, almost catatonic jungle boy stood in front of him.

"Father Wolfe. Am I glad to see you!" As Larry Curtland got up from where he had been sitting on the cot, he looked as though he might deflate and leave his clothes hanging in air. As though this was all he had waited for and now nothing else mattered. "They won't believe me."

"Father. Larry." Lieutenant Higgins was opening the cell door. "Come down to the lawyer room. We can't talk here. And the ordinary visiting rooms aren't adequate for this."

The two-story jail from the inside looked like an oversized shoebox. Two offices in the very front as you came up the stairs from Landor Avenue, with the visiting room off to the right, and the cells to the south along what looked like an endless corridor from behind the offices to the back of the building. More rooms—offices?—upstairs? In the basement? There were steps going down—to what, a parking garage? Probably not with all of that parking space in back.

The room Higgins ushered them into was a perfect cube. A box. And although apparently clean and painted almond, seemed hesitant to offer its services—for no discernible reason. Three no-nonsense chairs. A small, already tired desk.

The lieutenant led the boy in. Father Wolf followed. As soon as Larry turned around, the priest reached out of nowhere and gave the boy a bear hug. Strong, like hot new-brewed Starbuck's coffee.

"Won't believe what, Lar?" he whispered in his ear.

"That I did what I said I was going to do." His usually neatly parted red hair was wildly disheveled. But he looked Father Wolfe straight in the eyes, as though he wanted to reach out and force the priest's whole being to listen to him. Not truculent. But demanding. And their everyday greenness now seemed to be as distant and deep as the sea to the priest.

"And what did you do?"

"I killed my father."

FIVE

Dear Chollie,

It's five in the morning. And I shoulda—it's rilly just a lot of fun in writing to you to exercise myself in all the various and sundry solecisms and sandhis that I gotta continually exorcise on the tykes' papers—gone back to bed. But too much is brimming over.

Where did I ever get this idea of writing to you—now that you are gone to God these three years now? And yet I find this letter-writing the only way, often, that I can concentrate. And pray. How wonderful the whole Mystical Body of our Christ! Something the Catholic Church has cottoned to all down the years, our ability to talk to anyone who has gone on to meet God and is only too ready to tell that good God our needs and hopes and dreams from right there with Him, one with Him, unfettered, free. And so many non-Catholic Churches have jettisoned this wondrous truth.

So I'm putting my money where my mouth is since that's just what I keep telling the tykes in class. They so often lose themselves in distractions when they work over a subject orally. But when you write, you have to force yourself to concentrate more accurately on what you're doing especially when your brain is working fuzzily-wuzzily as mine is now. "And writing (maketh) an exact man." Bacon, was it? Was that—I guess it must be ADD—those are the letters, aren't they?—the reason for my difficulty in concentrating. Attention Deficit Disorder? Still mentally gimpy after all these years. Like, I guess, all the rest of Adam's chillun? Kinda.

Anyway.

Two things stand out like fresh blood on a white sheet—like that ultra-impressionistic (is that the connoisseur's word for it?) picture in the San Francisco DeYoung Museum we saw years ago. You saw this big painting, four feet wide and six feet high—jet black, shiny. In the middle there was a shapeless blob of diaphanous white, and partly over that and partly over the contiguous black was a blob of bright opaque blood-red. You poked me in the ribs—I was caught up in something on the other side of the room—and you said its title should be "Auto Accident at Night." And when I went up to read its title, that's what it was called. I laughed, even though I didn't understand the fun. I grasped it only years later when I saw the results of a real auto accident at night.

The first is that when Larry—well, yeah, I had better tell you that twenty-five little old minutes ago I finally finished talking with a student by that name whom the local gendarmerie have detained under lock sans key at our Jordan Street slammer—told me he killed his father, he said it looking straight into my eyes. Without fear. Without sorrow. Cold. Without hesitation. Without shame. Right then—and now—I see the wildly wrong in it.

You just don't say "I killed my father" the way you say "I had a Big Mac for lunch." But that's the way he said it. And that's the way he looked.

Just as coolly he told me why. Logically. Simply. Like a class in moral theology. My responses were quietly and calmly put aside as though I had not even opened my mouth.

And the second is that when we finished talking—we spent maybe an hour going back over and over the whole business—Lieutenant Higgins told me that yes, Larry's father is very dead. And when the police arrived, they picked up off the floor the gun Larry had used.

But there are no bullet holes in him. In his father's body. In Doctor Peter Curtland's body. Not one. But there are six casings in the room on the floor next to the body. Big .45s. And they all came from the gun Larry had in his hand, a big Clint Eastwood long-barreled Colt revolver.

Larry knows this. And he has no explanation for it. And he still says he killed his father.

Our talking went nowhere. Save that he was able to get it all there on the table. And quiet down. When we took him back to his cell, he was asleep on his cot before we got to the doorway.

Larry had been one of the most concerned-about-others kids you'd ever want to meet. Happy. Affable. Casually and sincerely friendly. To everyone. The antithesis of this now-frigid person we still called Larry Curtland.

Tell the Lord Jesus to send us His Spirit. Lean on Him—you're close enough. There is a key to this insanity here. Somehow I wonder if it's up to me to ferret it out.

I mean, who did kill the un-good doctor?

Am I supposed to resolve all this? Including Larry's left-handed approach to morality. Ooops, forgot for a second there that you are a southpaw, Chollie.

I don't know where to begin. Or even if I should try.

Should I?

Luke

SIX

"Father, remember that day three months or so ago?" Over and over. Like a carousel. Luke was running what he had heard and seen at the jail over and over in his mind. Over and over. Like a revolving door.

He should, he knew, go back to bed. Back? It seemed so long ago. But he just sat there mutely staring at the computer monitor.

"We had had all that rain. And Joey Pachko and I came by to waste a little of your time while we waited for a lull to run to our cars to go home. And Joey said how awful it was that the court had let that rapist who had just about killed the girl off with only a year in prison. And you had agreed that it didn't seem just. And then you had added that as awful as that crime was, the real crime of our times, you said, is the legalizing of abortion."

Yes.

"And Joey had out-loud wondered why. Since, after all, the girl—the woman—had to have some freedom in the matter. And you had simply said, 'But what about the baby? Does he have any choice? Where's the baby's freedom?'"

Gone.

"'If our country's freedom means anything at all,' you said, 'it means freedom for everybody. And no one but no one has the right to take that freedom away from anybody. Anybody. Child or man. Woman or boy. Black or white. Yet to be born or old man with one foot and an elbow in the grave. Life is life. It's God's gift. We just cooperate to bring it about. And care for it especially when it is weak or helpless or

28

close to death.' That's what you said, Father. You were really on a roll, excited. Like you were summing up your defense before the jury. It's probably almost word for word."

Right on. If it isn't word for word, it's certainly close. For once you learned your lesson well. Very well.

"And you hooked me with that, Father. Don't ask me how or why. We had heard all the arguments in senior theology class. Boris Bofford—he's got that flat way of talking when he lectures—had bored the whole business into our heads. Hey, that's pretty good. Boris. Bores us. *Bored*, like drill in. And *bored*, like ZZZZs city." Larry made as though he was grasping a Black and Decker and successfully holing the desk top he now stood in front of.

Well, Larry, you haven't lost your sense of humor.

"But somehow it never seemed to mean anything before. You know how you keep what you learn in class out there on the edge of your mind." His right hand flicked briefly at his temple. "Well, that's what I did. Until your words somehow sunk the hook in right past the barb. And there was no getting unhooked. You know what I mean?" And now he was miming the struggle with the imaginary pole that had a huge fish at the end of the line just the other side of the desk.

"Yes." *How could I miss it?*

"And then two weeks ago your words changed from fishhook to fuse. A fuse that touched off an explosion that blew the world apart." Larry looked Father Luke directly in the eyes as his hands empathetically exploded apart in front of him. "Pretty good metaphor, hunh?" He should have smiled, but he didn't. It was a throwaway.

"Yes." *You do have it all together. You do.*

"Because I suddenly saw what you said against the backdrop of Father Pete's ethics class last year. The end *does* justify the means. A good end. A good means. The end justifies the means. The end: no more murdered babies. The means: the same way we ward off an aggressor: slug him before he slugs you. The pre-emptive strike—isn't that what we learned in sophomore history class? Block out the safety before he gets his hands on the ballcarrier. Drop the atom bomb before the bad guys can kill millions of American soldiers." Larry's eyes glittered as he stared at Father Luke: he had made his telling argument. Knock it down if you can. If you can.

The jail conversation ran over and over on an endless tape in his mind. The square room. The unenthusiastic desk and chairs. The insouciant color of the walls. Was he somehow responsible for what this boy had done? Did his own possible guilt even matter now? Did it matter more than anything else?

Luke had pointed out that murder was not a good end. And the boy might just as well not have heard the words. As though the priest had not even said them.

He had explained with Robert Bolt's Thomas More that you can't throw out the law just to achieve a good end. He had reminded him how wrong Brutus was in killing Caesar because he was on the path to enslaving Rome. He pointed out the absurdity of offing anyone and everyone who was on the way to lend death a hand.

And Larry had gone back to, "But you would do anything to keep someone from killing me, wouldn't you, Father?" His bright green eyes drove right into the priest's consciousness.

"Of course." Where could this argument go from there?

He seemed a different person from the little-kid-like boy-man who had seemed to enjoy every moment of life. The same vivacious Larry Curtland, but somehow now no longer quite the same. Skewed. Like a fun-house mirror.

SEVEN

How to put this new Larry Curtland in focus? His mind leapfrogged back. Three weeks, four? It had been a Wednesday, because the students had been antsy after coming back from an assembly that had urged them against drunk driving.

"Father, you never call on Al." Larry pulled half out of his seat to the left and pointed at the huge blond potato-like body who sat next to him—whose rubicund apple cheeks made him a perfect model for a painting of a Munich burgher deep into his mug of Löwenbräu beer with his clay pipe lying alongside. It had been Larry Curtland teasing his best friend, Al Flyte, the biggest and shyest senior in the school. What an incongruous pair!

"You're always needling me, Father. I'm not the only genius in here." Larry's face was lighted with sarcastic laughter: he *knew* he was right then and there running the whole show: the whole class was attentively enjoying the repartee. "You should call on the other brilliant people in here—like Al."

"I thought Al did an excellent job of reading Hamlet's lines just now, didn't you, Jim?" He turned to Jim Hadeen. Jim sat on Al's window side.

"Sure, Father. Al always reads good."

Father Luke, turned to Jim, lowered his head and with a mock frown looked up at him across his eyebrows. "Um, *well*."

"Um, well." Jim's tone had perfectly mimicked Father Luke's, and he had lowered his head and with a mock frown looked across his eyebrows at the priest.

Al enjoyed reading aloud. And he wrote like a professional. But somehow attention drawn to him or the need for him to think publicly turned him shy and blushing.

"Well, Lawrence, since *you* are so brilliant, why not tell us precisely what that last line means, the one Al just now read with such brilliant dramatic emphasis?"

"Umm—what line was that, Father?'

"See if you can find it."

"You mean, 'The lady doth protest too much, methinks'?"

There's Billy Higgins surfacing again!

"Right on the button."

"Well, see, uh, this is, uh, Gertrude, Hamlet's mother, talking. And she's uh, talking about, about what Ophelia—her last name is Pulse, Father. Who else's pulse would you feel?"—he looked up at the old priest and smiled his thin-mouthed but infectious smile at the hackneyed class joke—"what Ophelia Pulse has just said to Hamlet when Hamlet has just made his gamey comment to the sweet young thing, you know, about—"

"Why not try again?" Father Luke looked out the window, touched a strand or two of white hair on his head, affected boredom with the class and a new interest in the jacaranda tree and the Jesus fountain outside. He walked to the windows wall to straighten the foresail of the *USS Constitution* model on the shelf.

"You mean she's not talking to Ophelia?"

"Who *is* she talking to?" Only pedants bothered with *whom* in this kind of give and take.

33

"I've got it. She's talking to the players that are putting on this show for the court."

"Really!" Father Wolfe's voice dropped an octave across the syllables. He turned back to look at Larry.

"How about Hamlet?"

"How about him?"

"She's talking to Hamlet."

"Is she?"

"Yes, and she is saying, is saying that the lady, the lady in the play in front of them, is making too much of how much she loves her king-husband."

"Too much?"

"Yes. She is repeating the words too often to really mean them."

"How so?"

"Besides with a needle and thread, Father?" Larry looked up from the text in front of him like a kindergartner who has just put together a word with his blocks on the floor. Another class joke. He smiled and looked around to see if the class was enjoying this as much as he was.

"Yes. Yes. Yes."

"Well, if she really loved her husband as much as she says she does, she would *not* have to tell him. Or she would have to tell him only once. And he would know that it was true by just the way she says it. Or body languages it." And with a squirm he body-languaged in his seat his pleasure in the right answer.

And that had been what? Three weeks ago? So open. So clear-headed. So free-spirited. And now he was somehow intellectually constipated. Or was he? Something was missing. He was not catatonic. But a very different Larry Curtland.

EIGHT

Without any sleep, he knew Monday's classes would be a briar patch. Nettles. A foray with a jumping cholla. Scratch here. Scratch there. Everywhere a scratch scratch. Behind his eyes. At seventy-eight he needed his sleep more than he had when he was forty. Or fifty. Far more. But when he remembered to go back downstairs to hang up the car keys to #5, the pale green Neon, the seven thirty-two on the clock meant just time for a shower and a cup of coffee and a déjà vu shave. And yes, he had better brush his no-longer-pearly whites, too.

Ten minutes later he was on the way, briefcase tucked under his arm and coffee cup in hand.

Jesus, walk me over to school and stay there with me or I'll never make it through the day.

He shuffled along the breezeway over the chapel cloister from the Jesuit residence to the school, stifled a groan when the arthritis climbed on for the ride—and then with an effort lengthened his stride.

He was in the classroom a little before eight. And his head seemed to have developed a large protuberance at the back that was somehow tumorous. Swollen. Frozen. Dead in the water. He reached up to feel the swelling. But it wasn't to be found on the outside. Inside was where the sleep-deprived pressure pushed and shoved.

"Hey, Father." Just as he was opening the door to Room 102. It was Norm Balinski. Norm's glasses had rims as big as coffee mug bases. His voice conjured up a tugboat's warning hoot. "I finished my paper for religion class, but our printer is kaput, and I wondered if I could run it on one of your computers. Have to explain all about David's big sin to Bofford—uh—Mister Bofford. It reads like an R-rated movie. Nothing new in the sin line, hunh, Father?" Norm smiled his face-stretching gap-toothed smile. "I got the three-five disk right here." The disk he held up was yellow, like a brand-new VW Beetle's.

Father Luke's head was too heavy to think of an easy way to tell Norm that it was *"have got"* or just plain *"have."* "Sure. Be my guest." He put his battered briefcase down on the student desk closest to the door and gently jackknifed himself into it. He pulled out a file folder full of student papers and a green pen.

"Where do I turn this on, Father?" Norm was in the front of the classroom on the side opposite the teacher's desk. Father Wolfe was half out of his chair to show him. "Oh, down here. David and Bathsheba. Lust. Times haven't changed much, have they, Father?" Again. It somehow wasn't really a question. "Like whatshisname in *Hamlet*. The guy who kills Hamlet's father to get the queen's body."

"Umm, no. Claudius."

How had Brinkley so suddenly come up with such an astonishingly professional style? His sentences were usually labored and gravid with solecisms. Father Luke turned to the computer next to him and www-ed *pinkmonkey.com*. And *Hamlet*. And there it was, word for word. No, not quite. He had put in that extra comma here—and there—and left out a capital. Carelessness? Or to seduce his teacher into thinking it was his usual untidy work? Why play such games?

"Just like a soap opera, hunh, Father? Only it's really not very clean." Norm chuckled in the awareness of the humor he had just committed. As though he were accommodating an old friend who was really a little slow on the uptake. The laugh sounded like an 1920 Ford truck trying to shift gears.

Father Wolfe became, suddenly, conscious that his gelled mind was far away from Brinkley's purloining ways and was again taken with the age-old story of David, God's Chosen One. His purloining fall into the humanness that brazenly blew away the spark of God's life just to cover his theft of Bathsheba, the woman who was not his to take.

NINE

"'Lar, c'mon with us tomorrow.' That was Rita. And that was last Friday, Father. Here at Kino. In the mall." The school mall between Father Wolfe's classroom building and the gym, the mall with the grass and the reticent fichu trees and the bossy grackles and the happy but out-of-place fountain that seemed ill at ease. And the pigeons that quickly scavenged the droppings from the young male lunches. And the mockingbirds that happily took over in the evenings. Tony gestured toward the doorway at the east end of the hall. Somehow he let you know that the pointing hand was only an extension of that huge football shoulder.

They were standing at the door of Father Luke's classroom. Break time after second period. Father Luke had asked Tony to stay after to backdrop the whole Larry Curtland scenario.

"We were over there by the gate. The nearest one by the parking lot." Tony again raised his huge left arm and half turning pointed to the northeast. 'What's tomorrow?' Larry asks. 'The day after today, Lairee.'" Tony sang the name a little the way he thought Rita had and ended up high on the staff. "She's fluttering her eyelashes like some big movie star." He fluttered his as he dead-panned at Father Luke just three feet away. "And she was looking at Lar from way behind her eyes. Did you look at them when you met her last night, Father? They're as unsettling as a waxed and buffed black Honda finish. And against that white skin of hers."

"Yes, she is very pretty, Tony." *And yes, he had caught those unsettling eyes. But there is a real depth in those black eyes, too, Ton.*

"'Rita has talked me into joining her Pro-Life group,' I chime in. 'They're going over to the abortion—um—clinic on Sixteenth and Hibiscus and protest. You know, say the Rosary. And walk back and forth in front of the place. Just far enough away so we don't break that stupid law.'

"'Well,' says Lar, 'I'm really really dead set against abortion, but I don't really think I have the time to—'

"'Oh, come on, big boy.'" Rita was doing her Mae West 'Come up and see me sometime' imitation now. "'What you got going tomorrow that's more important than saving a life or three?' She must have been grinding her right hip. And Tony was doing his best at a fair if awkward imitation.

"You know Lar, Father. He comes up with that little-boy 'Aw, Rita.' But she just says, 'We'll pick you up at your place at seven-thirty. OK?' And Lar is horrified. 'On Saturday?' 'Sure,' Rita drawls. 'Like, who wants to sleep when you got something fun to do?' And she laughs that throaty laugh of hers. Like the water in the mall fountain."

Doesn't anyone say have got *anymore?*

TEN

"What's really bothering me, Father, is that the whole Curtland business is just one big mess. One big mess. One hell of a big mess."

Ever since he had met Amy Halloran on the arm of Hal Duchesne at his senior prom, he had wondered what Big Man On Campus Duchesne had seen in her. As she stood on the other side of her desk, she seemed just enough overweight to make her pleasantly rotund. She was certainly plain-featured, if certainly very feminine and petite, with a neat round head that reminded him of an over-enthusiastic softball, with bright and disconcertingly green eyes on the front over a thumbtack nose, framed by a flaming red hair halo that was almost as short as a man's haircut. Like a wig. Now, she seemed to swallow her words as though she was afraid that whoever was listening would actually hear what she was saying and understand them. Apparently marriage to Hal and three children had brought out who she really was.

And right now she was Sergeant Amy Duchesne. And Father Wolfe was very much aware that she was in charge of the Curtland case. She had introduced herself with that byte of information.

"Doctor Curtland is indeed very dead, Father. And Larry unhesitatingly says he killed him. But, Father, there is a suhlight diffewculty." She looked straight into his eyes as she accented the second syllable of the final word.

Is she clowning? Or is this really the way she talks?

"Father, there are no bullet holes in the body. In the body of Larry's father. Doctor Curtland's body. No place. Not in his toes or his chest or his left ear. No bullet holes. And there are the shell casings we found in his office. Forensic insists they were fired by the gun Larry had in his hand when we apprehended him." All this all over again, exactly as Lieutenant Higgins had explained.

Why is she telling me this?

"Well, what *did* kill him?" He chuckled in his best avuncular fashion. "Isn't that what I am supposed to ask? I *am* supposed to ask, am I not?" He had to be wearing his English teacher hat to come up with that one.

"Father Luke, I really do wish you could be a little serious about all this."

And I thought you were the one doing the clowning.

"We right now as of this very moment at this point in time have absolutely *no* idea. That's why I asked you to come down here right after you said your last class ended this afternoon. Do *you* have any idea?"

He felt giddy. All through the classes that day, all through the sophomore classes that tested them on whether they had read "Chiquita's Cheese"—the short story in the literature book the students were supposed to have read over the weekend—and then going over the assassination scene in *Julius Caesar* and then trying to get the seniors involved in the *real* reason Hamlet postponed the killing of his uncle, he had nursed like a neon-ed billboard in the very front of his head the great beauty of the final bell and a large siesta till that evening's Mass with his brother Jesuits. And

41

Amy had phoned and pleaded with him to come to her office at the Jordan Street jail.

They were back there again. Larry had not killed his father. But he had *said* he had killed his father. He had said he *wanted* to kill his father. And it certainly looked as if he wanted to kill him. And he had said he wanted to kill him. And that was evil. Monstrous evil in itself. Thumbing your nose at the good God Who gave life as His most precious treasure. *If you are even angry with your brother, you have already killed him in your heart.* But somehow he had not followed through. Somehow God had stepped in to shield him from that gruesome guilt.

Jesus, forgive him for whatever he did do. Wanted to do.

He stared at the picture of Sergeant Duchesne's children on her desk. *Who is taking care of them?* Swung his gaze out into the street to watch the evening flow of traffic on Jordan. "No," he said, and laughed a little laugh and looked evenly at her. "No, I have no idea."

"I know there are a lot of things that you cannot tell me, Father. You're a priest. I unnastan"—*Did no one say* understand *anymore?*—"that." She worried the rubber tip on her pencil into the desk top. "But is there something out there in the open that you know will help us? And, please, do not tell anyone what I am telling you. This whole thing is ridiculous."

"No, there isn't. And yes, it is. I know what Larry told me. And I am sure it was exactly the same thing he told you. But if you'd like, I will puddle around with his friends about all this. Maybe something will surface."

"Fair enough."

As tired as he was, he did *not* want to ask the question, but somehow it was inescapable.

"Sergeant, tell me how it happened, can you?"

"Didn't Larry give you the story?"

"Tell me how it happened."

Sergeant Amy Duchesne looked straight into Father Luke's eyes—was she questioning his sincerity?—made a too-red moue of her small mouth, turned around and, without a word, left the room.

Only a minute later she was back with a file folder in her hand. She sat down at her desk, opened it, looked blankly at Father Wolfe and then down at the paper in front of her.

"The composite from the various witnesses to the whole episode—Receptionist Carter, Nurse Huey and Nurse Gliddens—comes to this." Her voice dropped into a monotone. She seemed to be reciting the lesson she had learned the night before—to her fellow fourth-graders.

"Larry Curtland got out of the driver's seat of a red sedan—it turned out to be a 1999 Pontiac—he had parked in the lot in front of the clinic, about five spaces down from the stairs up to the office door on the second floor. As he got out, it was quite evident he was carrying a large revolver in his right hand quite openly by his side.

"Mrs. Carter—the parking lot is right below her office window—immediately called his father who had been in his office following an abortion a few minutes before. She also called Doctor Brandt. Doctor Curtland came right out of his office—apparently to confront his son—followed by Doctor Brandt from *his* office. With

43

Doctor Brandt right behind him, Doctor Curtland reached the door of the foyer—that's at the southeast corner—just as his son charged in from the front door at the northwest end. Doctor Curtland hesitated for a moment, to the surprise of Doctor Brandt, who bumped into him and bumped him into the foyer itself." Never once did she look up from the paper in front of her.

"Without hesitation and from across the room—it is approximately forty feet in length—Larry Curtland raised the gun from his side and aimed it at Doctor Curtland's chest and pulled the trigger. Six times. At the first explosion the doctor merely looked at his son and fell forward without speaking or making a gesture of any kind. And as his body fell, the boy altered his aim and emptied the gun into his father's back.

"Larry Curtland had then dropped the gun on the floor and just stood there, looking at his father's body." She continued to read as though it had all happened someplace in another universe.

"After a few moments—apparently of shock— Doctor Brandt jumped forward to touch Doctor Curtland's neck artery and shook his head. The two nurses and Mrs. Smedana who had just gone off duty as receptionist came to the door the doctors had entered by. The paramedics and police Mrs. Carter had nine-one-oned arrived within five minutes—both police and paramedics. When they arrived they found Larry on his knees next to his father's body."

Was he offering a holocaust to God?

"The paramedics immediately tried to revive Doctor Curtland, even though Doctor Brandt—quite convinced that he was gone and beyond recovery—had made no effort to revive him. They did take the body to St. Mary's Hospital Emergency. There he was pronounced dead a little while later.

Father Wolfe stirred himself in his chair. The monotonic voice had him drifting off—he was so very tired—in spite of the fact that he really wanted to store away in his mind each iota of what she said.

"The police—an Officer Matthews was in charge—brought Larry Curtland and the gun here—to the Jordan Avenue jail."

"Has forensics discovered anything new? Anything out of the ordinary about Doctor Curtland's body?"

"No, Father, nothing." Her voice was back to normal again. "Except"—she laughed a surprisingly deep laugh as she looked right at the priest—"that he had picked up a bad case of fleas someplace. His body was covered with flea bites."

"Flea bites?"

"Flea bites."

"Well, that doesn't help much. Would it be a good idea, do you think, for me to see Larry again now that I am down here?" He felt as though he were trying to coax a frightened freshman into identifying a gerund on a past test. But Amy apparently felt none of his reluctance.

ELEVEN

"It's all pretty logical, Father." Larry Curtland had gotten up from behind the desk and was pacing back and forth in the little office. Sergeant Duchesne had again allowed them to talk in the more relaxed lawyer conference room.

"Well, if it is, then all of us Catholics—all pro-life people, for that matter—should go around shooting up all those abortionists and bombing their clinics. You're telling me that another Civil War is what is called for."

"That's exactly what Harry Smathers told me. More than once. He'd lean up over his desk and then whisper in my ear something like 'At least we Baptists are honest. At least *my* Baptist Church. Sure, abortion is no good. But the woman's got to have her freedom. You Catholics say abortion is just plain never no good ever. If you Catholics had any guts, you'd all go out and off every last abortion doctor you could find. Just the way you took on every Muslim in sight in the great and wonderful and bloody Crusades—which is one reason, my son, why you are never going to find *this* guy a Catholic. You Catholics get on your high horse about truth and the sanctity of life when you've got no power. And as soon as you get in the saddle, there's rape and pillage and the Inquisition and you burn Joan of Arc.'" He stopped in front of Father Luke's chair and looked directly at him, hands on hips.

Larry will make a great lecturer some day. In fact, he's a great lecturer already.

"Sure. I know he's got hold of a lot of half truths–"
"And a lot of whole untruths."

46

"—there, Father. But the words that grabbed me were 'If you Catholics had any guts, you'd go out and off every last abortionist.' Every last abortionist.

"You know where Harry's coming from, Father. He figures that the North took far too long—and we as an American nation—took far too long to free his ancestors. As a nation we should have wiped out slavery the moment the first slave stepped on our shore. No matter the cost. No matter who died as a result.

"And you know, Father, I cannot and could not answer that.

"Huh. And then you made us memorize—" For a moment the green eyes were on the way to a smile.

"*Asked* you to memorize—" Larry looked up and now smiled his thin-lipped smile.

"—that *Lepanto* thing."

"Chesterton."

"Yes. There's that line: 'It is he whose loss is laughter when he counts the wager worth.' So I do what is right and I get put in prison. So I end up executed in some supposedly civilized way after death row time. Well, the wager *was* worth it. I kept that man—my father—from killing any more kids."

I had hoped the kids would cotton to that line. But I didn't want them to swallow it whole like this.

"See, Father, I didn't pick up on any of the ordinary community service projects Kino offered." Larry was pacing again, talking to himself almost as though Father Luke were not there. "I went and poked around at St. Mary's Hospital. After all, my father *is* a doctor—no matter at the moment what kind. And I came to feel at home there. I met Sister Angela. She

47

must be about a hundred and fifty years old—wrinkled but so kind and gentle you wouldn't believe. She welcomed my help there as a volunteer in any which way. She was what her name said, an angel to me."

"A perfect example of an eponym." Father Wolfe smiled.

"Sure, Father." His voice sounded as though he had only then adverted to the priest's presence as he looked up at him. He had obviously missed something.

"And I got this cleared by Weasel—er, William—Wouk—the head of Community Service—here at Kino. For my Community Service Credit. So every day when I got finished with cross country practice or a meet, I would head down there and spend an hour or two wheeling people around, running errands, cheering people up, offering my help wherever anybody needed a helping hand. And most of my weekends. And after a while just about everybody there got to know me. And I could go just about anywhere—even places theoretically restricted. And one of these was maternity."

He stopped and stood looking at Father Wolfe—the priest looked very sleepy—to be sure he was still listening.

He was pacing again. "After wheelchairing mothers out to their car, I found out where all the newborns were and often went there just to look at them and laugh at them and wonder if I would ever have a whole roomful of my own and if I could maybe become an obstetrician or pediatrician for all these wonderful, cute, tiny, fabulous human beings whose lives were so fragile and needed the gentlest of care and protection." Larry stood still and smiled wanly at the priest.

Father Wolfe had gone mute. It was all so logical. And so skewed. Like a tête bêche sheet of stamps. Beautiful, but with at least one stamp upside down. Where could he reach in and turn the whole argument rightside up?

"And then Boris Bofford tells us in class one day about Father Lelso—one of your guys, isn't he, Father—a Jesuit? He goes—sometimes alone and sometimes with others, a couple of nuns and a handful of lay people—out and hammers on the nose cone of an F-16 and pours pig's blood all over it in their protest against war and our nation's policy of kind of being the world's traffic cop with bombings and bullets. And they end up in prison for a couple of years. And as soon as they are freed, they find a submarine and some more blood and end up in prison again. Their protest costs them—I can't think of any sane person relishing time in prison. And here am I a Catholic, urged by God to protect life wherever I find it, and I do nothing to stop the waste of four thousand-plus lives every day. How can I stand before God with bloodless hands if I do nothing to protect these innocents?"

"Larry, you can't just go around—"

"Father, I'm grateful that you come down here every day to visit. Well, this is even really twice in the same day, isn't it? Please keep coming. I've gotta talk to somebody who unnastans." Father Luke was too tired to correct him.

"But I find my arguments so tight I cannot escape them. And I really do not want to spend our time together re-hashing them.

"And next time you come—"

"Tomorrow if I possibly can."

"—is it possible to bring me Communion? After our senior retreat at the beginning of the year and George Lessing's awesome talk about the value of the sacraments and especially Holy Communion—that was right after Mass on the first day—I started going to Father Bill's Mass every day after fourth hour. And I have really missed the physical presence of the Lord Jesus each day I have been here."

Well, that is *a surprise, Lord.*

"Of course."

TWELVE

"Well, good evening, Father."

Father Luke had driven home from the jail—singing along with the radio on at ear-bursting volume, thumping the steering wheel, pounding his left foot on the floor—to keep from dozing.

Now, he felt as though he had been run through the wash machine spin cycle as he turned to face the voice. Fear doubled into his whole being. And he saw no reason. It was still light enough out, the sun at the moment taking its leave in a spreading warm glow of affection as it disappeared over the dilapidated three-story apartment building on the west side of Kennedy Drive. (When John F. Kennedy was assassinated, the city fathers—emulating other American cities—had decided that their patriotism and sorrow could best be expressed in changing the cowtown Main Street to the more sophisticated Kennedy Drive.) And the speaker—it was easy to see him as he faced that last smile of the sunlight—wore an unprepossessing rimless-glasses-decorated gentle smile.

"I hope I didn't startle you." And the gentle smile returned.

Father Wolfe had wheeled the five-year-old Neon into #5 Jesuit Faculty Parking slot and was just climbing out. He stifled a gasp—as he always did when he changed a long-held position. Probably just arthritis. *Just* arthritis? Lumbago? Rheumatism? Just old age? And then he grinned. "You *did*. I had been thinking of other things."

He had been thinking that he had arrived home just early enough to reflect on his homily for the community Mass—if he was able to reflect intelligently on anything any more today.

And he was baffled that his talk with Larry had been frustratingly simple and straightforward. Larry had been pale and somehow a little more disheveled than he usually appeared at school. But he was calm throughout their whole discussion. And somehow at peace when he smiled just before Sergeant Duchesne opened the door at the end, and said, "Yes, I killed him, Father. Nothing has changed. And I do not know how I can say this, but I am glad that I sent him to meet God." No, nothing had changed.

Luke had no answer for that. How do you conjure up the awareness that the ramifications of taking a human life are unthinkable? Full of more shudders than the wildest alien horror flick. And he had hugged the boy again.

Through the big plate-glass windows, he had watched Sergeant Duchesne escort Larry—the two red heads—back down the corridor to the boy's cell.

"Who am I talking to?" He smiled back a gentle smile to the round-faced man with the gentle smile. There was the *who/whom* thing again. *Whom* here, of course. Objective. Object of *to*. But not even English teachers talked that way. Even if they wrote that way. And orated that way.

"Dr. Brandt, Father. Dr. George Brandt. Greg Farrell's father."

"I should have recognized your voice."

Jesus, give me your patience. I need it with this guy: he just does not seem to understand. "Would you like to come into our parlor, Doctor?"

"No, this is just fine. If you don't mind." There was something unnerving about his simple words. As the overhead arc lamp ceased its dithering indecision and snapped on full, Father Luke was seized with the immediate impression that before him stood an animated M & M figure. Oh, he had a neck of course, and a head disparate from his torso. But in spite of his height—he was at least six foot four—he had short legs. And a you-gotta-follow-me paunch. And the happy—and—gentle smile that opened a mouth between the chin and an embarrassed nose.

"You know, Father, this whole business is pretty silly."

"You said it, Doctor. *You* said it."

"Is there something you would like? Something I can get you?"

"I have been offered bribes before, but never from an adult." He tried to smile, but was not sure if his face had made it.

"Oh, Father." His laugh sounded like a constipated machine gun with a virus hack—hahaha haha hahaha. G on the staff. "I just don't see why you can't bend a little." His rimless glasses glinted as he swung his face down from the light and faced Luke. "Jesus, after all, was always kind and gentle." *Except when you threw the money-changers out, Lord. And called the arrogant Pharisees vipers.*

"You do *not* seem to understand, Father." The doctor was warming to his subject. "All of the males in our family—yes, I know, Greg is not a blood relation—have gone to Harvard. I *know* that Gregory has more than enough intelligence to succeed at that prestigious institution. But he will never matriculate there if he fails your class and fails to graduate." The voice was getting higher and tighter, and the words were almost stumbling over one another in their anxiety to be heard. "I am willing to do anything— anything—to rectify this his current ability to attend." The quiet voice was out of the scabbard now: it wore a keen, threatening edge. "The utter shame, the infamy attached—when all that's needed is your understanding and cooperation, Father." Dr. Brandt moved closer.

"I don't either, Doctor—see why I cannot bend a little. As soon as Greg does his work."

The machine gun laugh again—soft, polite. And then he stumbled, reaching out to Father's arm for support. Luke felt something scratch his bare arm below his short sleeve. And pulled back.

"Why, Father, I could have killed you." His glasses glinted.

"With a scratch?"

"I could have had anything lethal. I could have in that instant popped a bubble into an artery that would have had you dead in three seconds. I'm an expert with a hypodermic, Father." The voice had returned to its gentle mode. Clinical. Professionally distant.

"But you wouldn't have, would you, Doctor? Doctors do not kill. Doctors save lives. Isn't that what that Hippocrates guy said way back there in the fourth century? Before Christ."

"You have the wrong man. I am a full-fledged MD. And I save lives by the score every day. The lives of the unfortunate women who are caught in a hapless pregnancy. I give them new hope. And freedom. Drop over to our ultra-modern clinic, Father. On Sixteenth."

Father Luke was suddenly seeing in front of him what his mind's eye paralleled to the crowing rooster that had ushered in the newscasts before the main feature at the movies when he was a boy.

"All perfectly legal. I am—well, I *was* Peter Curtland's partner. And his half-brother—you see, our mother re-married after she had Peter. He married my—our—distant cousin—someplace out there—Eudora. Beautiful lady. We'll—I'll show you how it's done. Or we can show you a video. Or three. If you're too squeamish for the real thing! As I say, it's all perfectly legal, of course, as you Catholics well know." He smiled his soft and gentle smile. All was relaxed again.

"You aren't really suggesting that I witness an abortion, me, a Catholic priest. Don't you know what the Catholic Church says about abortion?" His anger had pushed out and beyond his sleep-deprived near-stupor.

"Oh, Father, you must try to be open-minded. This is the land of the free, after all." And he smiled.

"You're an anomaly, then? A life-saver who kills? A murdering savior?"

"Oh, Father. We cherish the life and well-being of the woman in trouble."

"Maybe *oxymoron* is a better word—the juxtaposition of antithetical words. The word you want, Doctor, is *oxymoron*." Father Wolfe was aware that he was losing control of his anger and being immature in the way he was speaking the obvious truth. And pedantic.

"Oh, Father." Dr. Brandt smiled gently again. "There was nothing lethal in that scratch. Just a dab of nicotine. You will itch there for a day or two. Just a reminder. Nothing more."

"A reminder of what?" He suddenly felt weak. In need of food. And delicious sleep. "Doctor, skip the bribe. Are you—I can't believe this. Are you threatening me?"

"Oh no nonononono." The laugh. Longer this time. Louder: a higher caliber. "Nooooooo. Just hoping you'd want to reconsider Greg's mark. Let me repeat: we all want to see him matriculate at Harvard, don't we? Good evening, Father." And he quick-footed it to his black Lexus. Small steps, like a four-year old's. A brief wave and a gentle smile and a glint of light from his glasses and he was gone. In a quiet harmony of affluent valves and happy gears and soft leather.

Why doesn't he coax and threaten and bribe his son?

THIRTEEN

"Good evening, Father."

Mrs. Samantha Smedana—Father Luke sometimes wondered if her parents had given her such a name as some kind of shibboleth: only the right people would be able to pronounce it quickly and accurately, perhaps—ran the switchboard at the Jesuit house in the evenings. She loved to mother the members of the community. Her haggard features—her square jaw had slipped forward a little like an aggressive boxer's and the skin under her watery-blue eyes had sagged—belied the permanent smile that told all and every how happy she was to see them. There just were no bad days for Mrs. Smedana.

But tonight was a little different perhaps.

"Father, aren't you involved with that Larry Curtland business?" Her brow furrowed, but only for a moment.

"*Involved* is not quite the word. I am trying to give him a little support—to tell him somehow that no matter what he has done, we still love him."

"Well, that's pretty easy. I'm sure glad he done what he done." When she got excited Mrs. Smedana's grammar listed a little to starboard. Or perhaps she was parodying Marlon Brando's Terry Malloy *On the Waterfront* un-grammar. "With pleasure I would have finished off that"—she paused, it seemed, to make sure that Father knew she was running through the unladylike thesaurus of words that nice people never used in front of a priest—"awful man." She ran her open-fingered right hand through her already rumpled greying hair.

"Mrs. Smedana, murder mocks God Himself and His gift of life." Did that come from him? He felt sooo tired. Still, he shouldn't have been so gruff with her.

"Do you know what he done, Father?" *Mrs. Smetana, that word is* did. "Why, I can feel his throat in my hands right now. I'd strangle every breath he could breathe. Do you know what he told my daughter? He told Cynthia that"—she cast her eyes demurely on the desk in front of her—"that if she got in TROUBLE—he said it in capital letters—she could come to him. He'd give her ease from her burden— that was the way he put it—ease from her burden." Was she really strangling him in her mind as her hands wrestled with one another on the desk in front of her? "Free. No charge. Ugh."

"And when she did get in trouble—Father, she's only sixteen—the good"—Mrs. Smedana looked as if she were about to vomit—"doctor put her on his table here and tore her child from her and killed it. Without a word or even a wink at me." Mrs. Smedana now seemed to be beating the doctor's imagined head on the desk in front of her, methodically, satisfyingly.

"I knew none of this until I had to rush Cynthia to St. Mary's emergency a week afterwards—he had so botched the job that she was hemorrhaging. Just three weeks ago." With one last shake of the head in her hands, Mrs. Smedana was apparently satisfied, and dropped the imagined head into the wastebasket beside her chair.

"Yes, that was an awful thing to do, Mrs. Smedana. But Jesus tells us to condemn the act but never the sinner. You wouldn't really want to have killed him."

Couldn't he be more gracious?

"Oh, yes I would. And I had it all figured out. Peter Curtland had a bad heart. Well, anyway, it wasn't the strongest. I would have gotten hold of a Halloween witch costume, and jumped out from behind the door in his office. I work *their* switchboard from seven in the morning to three in the afternoon. And poof! he would have been a goner. Dirty man! But his son got to him first. Good boy! Why, I even had the outfit in the office the day the boy did his good deed for the day." *Would* have gotten the costume? *Had* the costume in the office? What was she telling him?

"Mrs. Smedana, did you don a witch costume and jump out in front of Doctor Curtland and scare him to death?"

"Oh, I wish I had, Father." Her voice took on the tone of a fasting football player at midnight plus one on a Lent Friday with a fresh In and Out Double Double smiling up at him. "I missed my chance. I saw Larry walking across the parking lot. With that huge pistol hanging from his right hand—he wasn't hiding nothing."

It's anything, *Mrs. Smedana,* anything.

"And I said to myself, Here's my chance. He'll come right through here on his way from his office. He knows his father quits exactly at five. And when he comes into that room, he'll let him have it. But I will surprise the good doctor just before he enters the room. And Larry will get the credit for the good riddance that I have done." And there was a great deal of enthusiasm in the *I*. "But I had only got my dress and cape on—not my hat—when Doctor Brandt came rushing in with a hypodermic in his hand—he had just stepped out of the abortion room, or maybe his own office—and that

59

goofy TV lady that I thought had left an hour before was there wringing her hands. And Arthur—that's Doctor Curtland's other son—with his funny paint gun in his hand was standing beside her. It seemed as if the whole city of Phoenix was there by the surgery door to welcome him as he ignored them all and stepped into the foyer. And collapsed."

"All those people were there just before the doctor died?"

"All those people." Mrs. Smedana looked briefly and owlishly at the ceiling. "Maybe there was more."

That's were, *Mrs. Smedana.*

"And you never got around to scaring him to death."

"Never had a chance to be the one to finish him off." Her aggressive jaw pushed forward just a little more. "No."

Too much too quickly. Father Luke's wake-sodden head seemed incapable of a valid action.

"Mrs. Smedana, why do you work in a place where you loathe the evil they are doing?" His larynx had cooperated with his vacuous mind to produce a question he really wasn't interested in being answered just then.

"I work the switchboard here. And there. It's the only kind of work I can get, Father." Her head stayed level. She raised only her eyes. It was her ace covering his deuce.

FOURTEEN

"My brothers in Jesus Christ, let us call to mind our sins." In spite of his weariness—perhaps because of it—suddenly God was somehow very much *there* in the chapel when he started the community Mass for the day in the Jesuit house chapel. They were all there, all fifteen of them. No, Gary had probably been held up with a special case at his law office downtown. And where was Barry? Still at St. Mary's probably, with one of the dying. And two of the scholastics—priests in training—were undoubtedly still out coaching on the soccer field. God was almost tangible in each of the ten who were there. With all of them. Together.

"Lord, take care of Larry Curtland. And his father. For this we pray to the Lord." The gravelly voice sounded like Gerry Atkins.

"Lord, hear our prayer."

Was that Phil who next prayed? "Lord, take from our laws and the hearts of our countrymen in the land of the free the curse of abortion. For this we pray to the Lord."

"Lord, hear our prayer."

"Lord, shine the love of Your Son into the hearts of all of our Kino kids."

He was so tired he could scarcely remember what he had said in his homily—in the Gospel Jesus had urged us to jettison fear—but at "This is my body" Luke knew that God's Son would take care of Larry and his father. Somehow. There was no feeling. But he knew.

Then, as he handed the chalice to John Bilshe— "The Body of Christ, John"—he was suddenly aware, almost tangibly, of Janey Peer. She was kneeling beside him at the Communion rail of old St. Philip's and they were waiting for the priest to come down the rail to give them Communion. And she suddenly laughed—he could never remember her laughing, just smiling—but now laughing and abandoned with a fullness and richness that seemed to be awash in all the happiness of the whole world. And just as quickly as the feeling had come, it was gone.

"Lord, may we receive these gifts in purity of heart. May they bring us healing and strength, now and forever." He particularly enjoyed this simple prayer after Communion at each of his Masses. Even now in his tiredness.

"Thanks, Luke." It was Bob, the quiet one with the brush greying hair and the sharp-edged but bright-blue eyes under black caterpillar eyebrows so much like Chollie's white ones. They were leaving the chapel together. "Your homily was full of faith for me." What had Luke said?

Instead of going to supper, he went to his room, collapsed on his bed and was instantly asleep. When he awoke, he saw on the bed-alarm that it was ten. And still dark. Of course. He stifled a groan, got up, went to the kitchen, where in the walk-in he found some thinly sliced ham, provolone and a tomato. He found a steak knife, sliced the tomato into thin, round faces, cocooned several slices of each between two slices of almost-hard white bread, washed it down at the scarred kitchen table with a can of Miller Draft, and went back to bed.

FIFTEEN

He awoke in a hot sweat. He had never been able to understand why novelists had their characters awaken in a cold sweat. Did the novelists themselves sweat cold? His sweats were *always* hot. He looked at his bedside clock. 4:00. Argh! Should he get up and say Mass? No, today he was saying the Mass at Mother Teresa at 7:00 for their teachers before they started school. Why had he awakened? A dream. No, he had to admit, it was a nightmare. He laughed a little. Out loud. He got up, put on his robe—the one he had bought at the Wal-Mart in Sandy Springs, Wyoming, when he and Charlie Waters had made their yearly retreat there, was it seven years ago now?—and Birkenstocks, and quietly went down the stairs to the kitchen. Corn flakes. Lactaid. A dusting of sugar.

Well, Father. I know this will be difficult for you.

Usually he dreamed few dreams and remembered little of them. But this one was etched there unforgettable.

I know you have been teaching forty-nine years. It was Gerald P. Sloan talking. Father Gerald Patrick Sloan, S.J. Principal Gerald P. Sloan. Boss Gerald P. Sloan. And Gerald P. Sloan had once upon a time— ummm—like thirty-odd years ago been a student in his senior English class. A very poor student. And whatever the semester final marks had been—he had never found the time or energy to look them up again—he knew they were not good. Not good at all. Much like his own high school grades.

And then Gerald had entered the Jesuits. And after his college courses he had come back to become a fellow English teacher at Kino. And then head of the department. Irony. Irony. Then when old Father Spaulding had died after twenty-seven years at the job, Gerald had become the Dean of Students. The disciplinarian. Irony. Again. And now he was Principal.

I have discussed this matter with the Assistant Principals and your Religious Superior. Gerald was a big man now. He had always had a large frame. But in the dream he was much overweight. So that his six-foot-three-inches carried a head that suddenly looked like a basketball. But a solemn basketball. And the desk he was sitting at somehow seemed like a doll house furnishing.

And after all this mature deliberation, I have decided that your teaching career here at Kino High School will terminate. Tomorrow. Before school starts.

He dropped two stale pieces of raisin bread into the toaster and rummaged around on the shelves above for some tea bags and then dropped one into a cup loudly labeled 49ers and filled it with scalding water from the water cooler. Irony.

That finis to teaching was, of course, what he feared. And he knew that fear was stupid. Stupid because he knew such fear was the antithesis of how he as a Jesuit should feel about the future. St. Ignatius wanted his spiritual sons to be indifferent to whatever God called them to. Not emotionally indifferent: no one could—or should even try to—effect that. But intellectually and willfully indifferent. Couldn't he still help others find God in a retreat house? He could still preach a retreat, hear confessions, counsel. Or a parish. Baptize and witness the big I Do of marriage and offer

Jesus to His Father on Sundays. Or could he? Maybe *they* wouldn't want him full time. But he could help out. He *was*, after all, seventy-eight. But he had a lot of energy left. Not as much as he once had, of course. Of course.

But whether he *should* fear or not, he did. Because although he intellectually knew he was a good teacher, that the kids liked his classes—usually more after the course when they began to realize how much they had grown than in the class itself when they were struggling—he often felt as he felt now that he was out of sync with the *new* things Gerald and his fellow administrators demanded.

They wanted longer class periods. And team teaching. And students teaching one another, often in groups. And freewheeling discussions that could go anywhere. And Power Point-generated Smart Board lectures. And—

His fun-and-games Socratic pedagogy to them was archaic. Old, but not wine or cheese old. Old like brittle bones ready to crumble. *Jesus, send me Your Spirit. I think I know the best way that I, me, Luke Wolfe can teach. But I don't know how to prove it. I do have a lot to learn. Of course. We all do. But I don't want to retire just yet. I come alive in the classroom. You know that.*

You know, Friend Jesus, that old raisin bread I'm enjoying right now isn't half bad toasted and signed with a bit of Smucker's strawberry jam to introduce itself to my gullet.

SIXTEEN

"See, Father, it must have been, like, a real shock to Larry."

Father Luke was opening the door to his classroom. He had just finished saying the Mass at Mother Teresa. Three nuns. Two women lay teachers. A short, sad-looking muscular man with a very long and thin neck, probably a teacher: he looked on the verge of correcting Father all through the Mass. Three girls. One very tall. Two *very* short. And as usual, he had tried to slow them down when they said the responses and the *Our Father* so quickly. With only moderate success. A disparate, almost motley group that with evident enthusiasm gave God their day by offering Jesus and themselves to His Father.

"Tell me again, Tony, what happened at the clinic."

"Well, we're over there on Sixteenth Avenue and Hibiscus. Uh, south—uh—southeast corner." He gestured extravagantly with that athletic left arm. "And the clinic is set back from the street, oh, maybe half a football field or so. And it's a two-story affair. You know, with stairs on either end of the building that make an el to accommodate the corner. And we're marching up Hibiscus and up Sixteenth and then looping back down Sixteenth and then Hibiscus and back up Hibiscus and—" Tony was now gesturing with both of his gorillian arms to the northeast. And turning corners and looping with his Italian hands.

"And we're, like, saying the Rosary. And Mrs. Poulos is leading us—Rita's mother. She teaches at Mother Teresa. You know, all fifteen decades. I mean, she teaches math. The Incarnation. And the Crucifixion. The Resurrection. All that.

"And we must have gotten to where Jesus rose when this guy on the second-floor landing starts booming at us through one of them"—*Argh!* Those, *Tony.*—"bullhorns. And he's got one of them"—Those, *Tony, those. You need an adjective instead of a pronoun!*—"funny surgeon's caps on. Green. Ugly. But he's wearing a jacket. Plaid. Don't know which clan, Father. Rita can probably tell you. But it's pulled back. And you can see the holster attached to his belt and the gun handle sticking out toward us. A big one. Like the one that spit-and-polish Marine that killed himself in *A Few Good Men* had. Big. A .45 maybe? And at first you couldn't unnastan what he's saying. And then it comes out loud and clear. He's saying stuff like we'll never stop him from doing his duty to keep women free to dump the burden of their children—yeh, I know it's hard to believe he'd be so disgusting—maybe really and down deep letting us know that he too thought the whole business was gross."

Tony turned to look fixedly at Father Luke. Did he want to be sure he was understood?

"And like, he wasn't in it for the money. And if anyone tried to stop him, they would enjoy the business end of his Big Bertha. That's what he called it. And he reaches down and pulls it partway out of the holster." Tony's hand was at his side re-enacting it now.

"Big, big gun."

"Yes. This is gonna be even harder to believe, Father. Right then he turns on this giant TV screen. Right in the middle of that second floor breezeway.

Huge. Maybe ten feet by ten feet. And on it, crystal clear comes this movie. As sharp and clear as Meld's geometry Smart Board diagrams and stuff. Don't know how they do it out there in the bright sunshine. And he explains to us as it goes along that he is showing us how kind and merciful he is in removing this troublesome growth from its mother. And the movie clearly shows him crushing the head of the baby he called a growth with those big blunt pliers of his. And he's smiling and being chatty all the time."

"A real friend."

"Yes.

"And then he tosses the body of the now dead baby into the trash can next to him—with a big Bio-Hazard sign on it. And right then next to me Larry turns to stone, staring at him. 'Dad,' he says. To himself, like. 'That's my father,' like he's seeing a ghost. And then he says, 'That's my father,' again. And when I look at him, there are tears running down his face. Like he's in some kind of a swoon. And even before the man up there stops talking, Lar stumbles off up Sixteenth— maybe he walked home. He lives up there near Happy Tree and Kennedy. Two miles, maybe. Or maybe he drove his little Z3 convertible. The one his folks gave him for his sixteenth birthday. No, he couldn't have: we picked him up and brought him over. Maybe I shoulda gone with him. But he seemed to want to be alone."

"Shocked him."

"Yeah. Somehow Lar never knew his father killed babies. Or maybe he knew but didn't know—didn't know what it *really* meant. You know what I mean?"

Tony gently touched the very center of his shaved head.

"Just an abstract idea."

"Yeah. Like the stuff we learn in class.

"Didn't see Lar again until the next day. Sunday. I went to his place to get primed on our calculus assignment. But Lar was someplace-else-ville. Like when we were sophomores and you underlined that Brutus wasn't himself when he thought about killing old Julius. I couldn't make much sense of what Lar was saying. But he did say something about 'all this evil.' I didn't stay long."

SEVENTEEN

So different had been Fr. Luke's exposure to Doctor Peter Curtland.

In the second week of the school year, late, late August, the Doctor and Mrs. Curtland had come to Parents Night. Along with the twenty or so other parents of fourth-period seniors. It was still warm, only slightly cooling from the 102-degree noon temperature, and it had seemed best to try to regale them with one-liners.

"Figures of speech? Sure. How about a pun? There was this butcher who backed into a meat grinder and got a little behind in his work." Hesitant laughter. Had they got it? And a guffaw or two. "And then there was the father who owned an orange juice company who refused to will his company to his son who had shown from his poor marks that he could not concentrate." He had looked straight at one and then another parent sitting in the student desks. Smiles greeted him. Some laughter. Did they get it? Was he pushing puns too hard? He gave them his best pseudo-sarcastic Tommy Lee Jones frown.

"What about alliteration? You all remember from Chesterton's *Lepanto* the line: 'There is laughter like the fountains in that face of all men feared.' And he had emphasized the *fountains* and the *face* and the *feared*. This met with a nod. And two smiles. Had they forgotten all this?

"How about some metonymy? 'Friends, Romans, countrymen, lend me your ears.'

"He wanted them after all, to lend him something more than their ears." Well, that got a guffaw from the bald man in the last row over by the window.

And then he had quickly outlined the course and how he hoped it would help their sons become professional in their reading and writing and speaking. The books they would be expected to read. Their analyzing of Shakespeare's tragedies—line by line. Trying to catch the figures of speech that exploded the meaning of the text. So that they would learn to read with accuracy. So that they would be able to be better men. So that they could come to meet Jesus Christ as he really wanted to come to us. With understanding. And intelligence. Clear and sharp.

And just as the bell rang at he end of the brief period, he was into explaining the airplanes and boats and posters and talking frog.

"I'm Dr. Peter Curtland, Larry's father." The little-boy dimples winked winsomely. "And this is Mrs. Curtland." After the bell, the couple had stopped on the way to the next class. Affable. Pleasant. The word *cosmopolitan* fitted them nicely. A pleasant-looking couple—she noticeably attractive in a quiet light-blue dress that said she was every inch a woman, and he in a quiet but clearly expensive beige jacket, white shirt and muted-red tie. Yes, there was the obvious gun in holster bulging his left-side jacket at the waist. Surprisingly, it hardly seemed out of place with his neatly groomed straight black hair and his rimless glasses and those dimples making him a shoo-in for a college professor who would make all the coeds go dreamy.

Packing the big handgun was legal in Arizona, of course, but Father Luke had never seen one like this before except when it had been strapped to the waist of a 250-pound helmet-less skinhead on a muffler-less Harley who had pulled up next to him at a stoplight on Williams and the I17 approach road and repeatedly gunned his engine for what must have seemed to him delicious blattings.

Pleasant, very pleasant. Mundane. Urbane. Sophisticated. All those nice words. The good Doctor Curtland had them all in his pocket.

"I hope Larry is doing well, Father." Mrs. Curtland seemed a little hesitant, aware of her place beside the obvious and somehow glowing success that was the Doctor. Demure. Not flaunting her obvious charm. Just letting it quietly glow.

"Fine. Just fine, Mrs. Curtland." And they were gone before Father Wolfe could ask Doctor Peter just what kind of doctoring he did. After all, at seventy-eight he wanted to know doctors he could put his trust in. And Doctor Peter had certainly and immediately seeded that trust in Father Luke.

But when the next morning he had asked Larry what kind of doctoring his father did, the boy without a pause looked out the window with, "Did you ever notice the way the sign on the tailor shop across Kennedy is just a tad crooked, un-level? Higher on the right side than on the left. *Todd Tailors*. The *s* is just an eyebrow higher than the first *T*." End of conversation. Why bother to ask about the cannon his father was wearing?

Of course, Dr. Brandt and his wife should have been there that evening too. But now that he thought about it, he had no memory whatsoever of Greg Farrell's stepfather showing up that evening. Or his mother. There had been no M & M figure with the gentle smile in the fourth-period class when Greg had English. Nor had he stopped by at any other time. Surprising—with his worries about Greg that would blossom only later in the year.

When he had collapsed in his room in the Jesuit residence afterwards, he was surprised by the Cactus Wren's hesitant *Boo-weep Boo-weep* from the garden below his window. Plaintive. Hesitant. Questioning.

Was there something he, Father Luke, had missed over there in the classroom that evening?

EIGHTEEN

"Hey, Father, there's a lady at the door." It was half an hour after Tony's prologue to the subsequent Larry Curtland acts. And Father Wolfe and the sophomores were deep into sentence analysis—trying to throw and hogtie plain old English grammar: nouns, adverbs, adjective clauses. Boring to the sixteen-year-old male mind, but necessary for a clear understanding of the language they speak.

"Jimmy G, you're just trying to distract all of us. Just tell us what construction this is."

"Father, there *is* a lady at the door." Jimmy's voice whistled a little, as he sat low—how did he scrunch down so far?—in his desk, his glasses much too large for his chubby pie-pan face.

Father Luke turned to the open doorway. Jimmy was right. There *was* a lady there. He walked to the classroom door.

"I just stopped by—sorry to interrupt your class..."

"That's perfectly all right..."

"Mrs. Curtland."

After a moment, he said, "Mrs. Curtland." His memory did a *pas d'action* to his dream: maybe Father Sloan was right about his decelerating memory. "Yes, we met at Parents Night." He should have remembered her demure urbanity.

It was the first period of the day. And it was Father Luke's particularly immature class of sophomores. The ones he sometimes thought of as The Class Least Likely to Grow Up—they seemed to act more like the kindergartners of St. Ignatius Elementary next door when they danced and skipped and poked one another and fell across the parking lot on their way to the big church than the almost adults the State of Arizona blazoned them as with their driver license. But there was a uranium lode of potential here. They needed constant attention that was exhausting. But there was the exhilarating challenge of trying to help them develop into God-fearing men, a challenge akin to trying to shut out the Dallas Cowboys with a team of eighth-graders. "The boys"—he glanced into the classroom where most of them had already taken up an animated conversation with their neighbors—"won't mind this little break in the routine." He touched the white tendrils on his head.

"I just stopped by to tell you how grateful I am for what you're doing for Lawrence."

She was a thin woman, small boned. And she wore some kind of a sheath dress that accentuated her svelteness. And she was handsome—her face was too narrow and the cheeks were too sharply etched against her eyes to be beautiful. But she was handsome. With light blonde hair that hung reluctantly but neatly over her ears. And Father Luke could immediately see where Mendel was right: Larry had inherited his red hair and green eyes from a mother that was blonde and a father with black hair. He would have to ask about his father's eyes sometime. At the moment Mrs. Curtland's were quietly focused on her shoes.

"I'm afraid it hasn't been much so far, Mrs. Curtland."

"Well, whatever you have been doing, please continue. He needs all the help he can get. He is certainly not getting it from the police." She looked up at him from surprisingly long lashes. *Are they her own?*

"Although I don't really know what they can do when he has confessed the murder. And his lack of any kind of remorse. And they undoubtedly feel he is a threat to every abortion provider.

"Father, should I come back another time?" She glanced quickly at the class.

"If you'd like."

It was as though he had not responded. She shifted her weight only slightly, but somehow she seemed to shift herself into another persona. She looked up, and held his eyes in her look. "I had often thought of doing what Larry says he did, Father. Peter had started out as such a bright and happy doctor right out of residency. You know, I'm going to cure the whole world. No more bugs. Cancer, die! AIDS, you no longer exist." She paused and looked past the class and out the window on the other side of the room. "Halitosis is a thing of the Middle Ages."

Why are you telling me this, Mrs. Curtland? Are you being sarcastic?

"And then I got sick." She was looking at the priest again, this time at his left shoulder. "They said it was terminal cancer. Maybe six months. And we needed every penny. And a very affluent young lady—you don't want to know her name—wanted an abortion. Just before *Roe*. Promised him so much long green stuff with presidents' pictures on it he said yes. For me. For my exorbitant hospital bills. And somehow after that—and especially after *Roe*—he became the champion of "women's rights." As though he had firmly closed a tight-fitting door on the room that said

76

no one had the right to kill anyone, much less defenseless babies. Hippocrates be damned. He's Catholic, too, Father. *Was* Catholic."

Somehow he could not stop her to explain that you didn't put on *Catholic* or take it off. Like a cap. Or a pair of shoes. Once a Catholic, always. That new life that is God's is your baptismal gift. Forever. For ever.

"He still goes to Mass. On Sundays. Did. Did go to Mass on Sundays. Never with me." She studied her left toe. It was making small clockwise circles on the cement.

"At first he couldn't bring himself to receive Communion. But after a week or two, he's right up there with the rest of us to receive the Body of the Lord. Since the 'Pope is old-fashioned.' His words, Father."

"I have no clue to how he managed to square that with his faith. No matter how often I tried to open the door, he refused to talk about it. It seemed as though he couldn't get over having done that first murder. As though it would involve making a mistake, committing a sin, as we Catholics put it. Saying I'm sorry." She looked directly up into Father Luke's eyes, her head sideways. And then she turned and stared down the hallway out through the front door to the cars passing on Kennedy. "And I often wondered if it was my duty to end the senseless slaughter he championed. Even with his kind of violence."

"Did you, Mrs. Curtland?" He suddenly adverted to the fact that he was absently scratching the arm where Doctor Brandt had nicked him.

"Course not." She looked back up at him, straight into his eyes, angry. "Of course not!" And then she was looking down. At her shoe again. She had suddenly gone quiet. "No matter what he has done, I still love him." And Father Luke noted that the part in her hair—somehow she suddenly seemed as small and as frail as a grade school girl—was absolutely and perfectly straight and clean. "Besides, evil doesn't solve evil.

"Father, please come to our house this evening. For coffee. Eight o'clock."

Before he could even think about whether he should excuse himself or not, she was gone.

Jesus, why wasn't she crying when she talked about this double tragedy? Why was she so cool? And aloof? And distant? What is wrong here? Will I ever understand women? No, of course not. Lord, take care of her. And Larry. And his father.

He stepped back into the classroom. "OK, guys." It was the voice of a coach expecting them to do better on the next blocking drill than they had on the last thirty-five. "Jimmy G, you were going to tell us how you knew that 'that the tomato is a tasty subject for discussion' is a noun clause."

He was talking quietly. The chatter subsided.

"Well," hesitantly, and escorted by a light whistle, "because it has a noun in it?" The class erupted in laughter.

NINETEEN

"Hear you're having trouble with Doctor Brandt. Over Greg." A Type-A person, John Finney had the unlikely combination of a skinny body and an over-sized billiard ball head. His blue, bright, raisin-size eyes looked straight at you over a huge soup-strainer waxed-to-stiletto-points mustache that stretched to the edges of his cheeks and obliterated his the mouth and dominated the goatee hidden beneath it: was it John's revenge against the Rogaine-proof Mojave on the rest of his head? He was a brilliant historian and an exciting teacher. But the total lack of hair enhanced the illusion that he was just what he looked like. All the glossy white skull lacked was a coat of glossy black enamel and a large white number. But reality returned with the nose that aped the Weaver's Needle—the rock that soared out of the desert north of Apache Junction.

"Yes."

"Disgusting."

"Who?"

"Well, Greg is no candidate for Most Affable of the Year Award either. Now, why don't they come up with an award like *that* for graduation?" John was being his usual exuberant non-sequitur self. This time in the teachers' lounge in front of the mailboxes. Second period was their mutual prep period.

"But it's his father that takes the proverbial cake in that arena—if you'll allow me to mix a metaphor or two. With a cliché."

"Did I miss something?"

"Probably." John snuffled. Was he laughing? It was hard to tell. "Did I tell you that we used to live

79

next door to him? We had our place there—over there on Ninety-seventh and Saguaro, new homes in the eighty-thou's—when he and his wife Mildred and Greg—*her* son from a former marriage, as I'm sure you know—and their four rottweilers, two Mercedes— should that be *Mercedes* or *Mercedes-es?*"—another snuffle—"and a Lexus entered the picture. With that display, I wondered why they weren't moving into a much pricier style of living."

He wiped the barren expanse above his eyes with a folded and soiled handkerchief that he produced from his right rear pants pocket as though it were a rabbit from a hat. John was always sweating. Father Luke absently wondered why no disgusting odor walked with that continual excrescence.

"But there they were. And hardly there a week when he made it *very* clear that he was trying to make time with my Mary. Well, Mary was friendly but distant at first. You know, pleasant but cool until he realizes he's on the wrong frequency. But he was wearing some kind of rejection-proof vest around his head—now, that's an anomaly, isn't it?—or is it?—and she finally had to make a declaration of independence in basic Angular-Saxon." He snuffled again and looked over his glasses into Father Luke's eyes to see if the old priest had perceived the pun. "And her cheerleader's voice. She came by that when she led the shouting at Mother Teresa's until she graduated. Well, *that* finally got to him. But the next thing the neighborhood noticed was that he had made a libidinous lunge for the lady on the other side. And that was his sister-in-law. You knew, didn't you, that that's his clinic partner's wife. Curtland."

"Mmmm."

"Yes, he is—was. Only there like maybe three months. And up went the For Sale sign. New Sun Realtors. Call Mimi. All that. Apparently they had found a habitat more suited to the money he was sluicing in from—the clinic." There was that minute pause before the politically correct word. "One of those places going for a couple mil on North Kennedy. You know. Eight-plus bedrooms. Game room. Pool large enough to bid for the Olympics Games.

"Father Luke, am I boring you? You look as though you are about ready to—"

"No. No. What you say is all very interesting." His lust for sleep must be showing.

"Huh. Well, did I ever tell you about the avid fisherman?" What did this have to do with Doctor Brandt? Finney's eyes took on a soft far-away look, just to the right of Father Luke's head. "Got himself out in the middle of Lake Bartlett—you know, that big lake way up to the northeast of Carefree—just at sunup."

"I know the lake."

"Dropped the bait and sinker and float. Then went for a cigarette. Cigarette-aholic, this guy. Alas, no matches. No *nada* to light it."

Father lacked the energy to drop the endman line. The question to prompt the gag line to this old, old joke. He smiled. Weakly.

"So what he did, he pulled out another cigarette. And threw it into the water. And thus made the whole boat a cigarette lighter." There was a slight pause. John looked the priest full in the face, and when he saw his smile, snuffled. Uncontrollably.

TWENTY

"Lord, I am not worthy to receive you, but only say the word and I will be healed." Larry Curtland was kneeling on the floor of the lawyer room and was saying the words together with Father Wolfe. The priest had come to the jail to bring Larry Communion as the boy had asked.

"This is the Body of Christ, Larry." Larry continued to kneel quietly as Father Wolfe closed the pyx that had held the Host and put it back in his pocket. Would people be scandalized that this boy, unrepentant of trying to kill his father, was receiving Communion? Father Wolfe hoped not: the boy from everything he had said seemed to be in perfectly good—if mistaken—faith. And he clearly needed the grace of the sacrament.

"May Almighty God bless you, the Father, and the Son and the Holy Spirit."

"Amen." Larry stood up. Then they both sat down, Lar again behind the desk.

"Lar, tell me again what happened."

"Well, I got out of my mother's Trans-Am and walked over to the stairs on the—um—south side of the balcony breezeway, went up the stairs and walked into the foyer there at the end.

"Just as I opened the door, my father came through the doorway at the south end of the foyer. I lifted the Colt. And just before I pulled the trigger, my father sagged a little." He paused. And Larry himself seemed to sag. Would he be able to make it through this?

"Then I pulled the trigger. Twice I aimed at his heart. And he fell to the floor. And the other four I aimed at his back." Larry looked down in front of him as though he saw it all again in his mind's eye.

There's a discrepancy there. Amy had said he had fired the gun as soon as his father came into the foyer. Larry says Doctor Curtland sagged a little even before he pulled the trigger.

"And then Doctor George was there right away. Checked his neck artery and shook his head. And I dropped the gun on the floor. And Mrs. Smedana came through the same door my father and Doctor Brandt had. And she had on some goofy kind of cape. She started to turn around to go back, but my brother Arthur was blocking the way and he had something funny that I didn't recognize in his hand and I later found out was my father's stun gun. As if there weren't enough people already, there's this huge TV lady and her camerawoman coming into the foyer from the north door.

"And then there were paramedics and police.

"Then they brought me down here." Larry paused as he returned to the jail room.

"Father, please get me the next book we have to read."

Father Luke couldn't bring himself to say, "*Asked* to read, Larry."

"*Too Late the Phalarope*?"

"Is that it?"

"I'll have it for you tomorrow."

"And Jesus? Bring Jesus?"

"I'll bring Jesus."

TWENTY-ONE

"I hate to keep asking you—well, me or another member of the department—to confer with us."

When Sergeant Duchesne had come to the door for Larry, a tall greying man in uniform had greeted him and asked him to come to his office.

Would he be spending a good part of his afternoons down here at the jail, each time talking to a different police officer? But then, it was only Tuesday.

This was Captain Parsons. *That* was a development, he supposed. From *Sergeant* Amy Duchesne and *Lieutenant* William Higgins to *Captain* Oscar Parsons. A slight movement that could have been the beginning of a grin flickered over Father Luke's mouth, and he absently touched the lonely hairs on his scalp to be sure they were in place: Parsons had never had the now dubious advantage of having been in his classroom.

"It may sound trite. But we are getting nowhere on this Curtland case." Parsons was exactly what you expect in a senior police officer. Quiet. Broad-shouldered. Neat. Eagle Scout. And by the time you had been with him for only a few minutes, obviously intelligent. He could have gone for a twin of Harrison Ford, save that his brown eyes were noticeably set a little too far apart, and he wore a thin, neat Zorro mustache. And that hair. It should have been straight and neatly parted. Instead, it was ebulliently curly. Unsettlingly out of control.

But his office reflected his mind if not his hair: neat, orderly, ready for the unexpected.

"And I do not want to talk to you about it on the phone because with these new phone systems you never know who might be listening."

"My classroom phone is on this same line with my Jesuit residence phone."

"That's what I mean. But we found this." He stood up and walked across the room to a closet. What he lifted from a shelf he brought over to his desk, carefully unsealed the plastic forensic document band and laid it on his desk. "This was in the closet that opens into the murder scene room." Together they unfolded what was there: a black cape, a 23-inch high black conical paper hat, a sharp wart-heavy putty nose—a Halloween witch costume. It was all crumpled and looked as though it had been quickly kicked into the storage area where it had been found. "Mean anything?"

"Only that Mrs. Smedana, Mrs. Samantha Smedana—I'm sure you know she works at the clinic as a receptionist—told me that if she had ever wanted to kill Peter Curtland, the easy way would have been to scare him with a halloween costume. Because he had a bad heart no one would suspect."

"Do you think that—?" The Captain dusted his mustache with a fond left forefinger.

"No. Although she is quite public in her assertion that she had partially donned the outfit by the time Larry arrived. And she certainly is vocal about her stark lack of affection for the deceased."

Captain Parsons puffed out his cheeks, walked around to the other side of his desk, sat down in his capacious chair and somehow pulled out an invisible plug that metamorphosed him from the Hobbes—in the old *Calvin and Hobbes* cartoon strip—that only Calvin saw to the doll that everyone else knew.

Father Wolfe folded slowly into the chair across from him. What was there to say?

"Father, the only reason we don't put this case on a back burner—" he fiddled with a button on his shirt; it was clear he did not want to face Father Wolfe—"is that Larry Curtland keeps insisting that he only wishes he *had* killed his father and that if he had it to do over again he would. And Judge Patterson has decided that he is therefore a threat to all abortion doctors—butchers, in Larry's lexicon.

"And none of the other leads lead anywhere." It was a final if redundant statement.

Father Luke knew the problem. And understood. "Precisely."

"Maybe Peter Curtland just dropped dead." Captain Parsons seemed to have forgotten that Father Luke was there. "And just maybe none of all of these folk who wanted him dead did the deed. And on the other hand, maybe one of the many people in that room when he died murdered him."

"But that still leaves Larry in jail."

Captain Parsons looked up from the intriguing button and touched his mustache as if he wanted to be sure it was still there. "Yes. That still leaves Larry in jail." He stood up and reached out to shake hands. "Do what you can for us, Father. For him—for Larry."

"Has anything more come to light? Can you help me?"

"Not really, Father. Just the six empty bullet shells. And the flea bites. And the fact that five people in that room would gladly have killed him. And had the means right there. Besides that, *nada*! He opened his hands on the desk as though he were the priest about to say the first prayer at Mass.

Is the good Captain completely candid here?

"Can I see him for a few minutes?" Back in the classroom he would have insisted on *may I* from one of the students. Well, this wasn't the classroom. Did anyone else worry about those nuances?

TWENTY-TWO

Twenty-three to nineteen. Third quarter. The Jayvees had yet to really warm up—even though ahead by a few points. There were four, no five, of his sophomores on the team, three of them out there on the court now.

Was Billy Erskine holding them back? They certainly weren't running and gunning in their usually happy-go-lucky play plan. As young as he was— hardly out of college—Billy certainly had turned out to be an exciting history teacher and a warm and manly and demanding coach for these younger basketball players.

It was one of Father Luke's nights to prefect an extra-curricular activity. So many other things that had to be done! Would that he could quietly sit in the stands and correct papers, but he found the situation too distracting to really get anything done. He looked across the gym to where Joe Burl and Annie Summers were doing just that. Annie looked up just then, scanned the gym situation, caught sight of him and waved. He waved back. Somehow that triggered something in Joe. And he looked and waved. And Father Luke waved back to both of them. Both single, still. Was there something special going on between them? Apparently. They'd make a good family. With thirteen or so children as buoyant and happy as they were. Well, that was how many he himself would have wanted—at least. Was he projecting his quondam dreams into the lives of others? What if he was? Father Wolfe smiled.

Another goal for Kino.

And he was back in the St. Luke gym the night of his best game ever. He had been really hot that night. Fifty-five points. And altogether the Thirties—he couldn't remember why they didn't call them Jayvees—he knew of course that he weighed no more than 130 pounds—back in those high school days— had pushed the score supersonically beyond anything they had done before. And the other team—was it Jefferson Commercial?—had kept pace only slightly behind. Until three seconds before the final buzzer. The score was 98 to 92. He had been fouled—a heavy hand across his right forearm—as he went up from under and behind the basket. It made no difference whether he made the free shots. But the stands wanted the century.

"Good evening. Father Wolfe?"

The priest was in mufti as he stood at the end of the stands. He found himself looking at a very young man in dark shirt and fungus-gray jacket. And bright green tie. "Yes, I am." He smiled. He wasn't quite sure why. "What can I do for you?"

"You don't remember me, sir." *Well, he's probably not a Catholic who would have said "Father."* "I graduated from Kino. In '97. But I never had you."

"I remember your face. But your name?" There was no response.

"What brings you back to Kino?"

"I came to interview you."

Father Luke laughed. "Well, interview away."

"I'm from the *Weekly Standard*." Father Luke suppressed a frown of disgust. The *Weekly Standard* was the Valley's ultra-liberal free paper, replete with advertisements and personals offering sex metropolitan

and varied. Occasionally they headlined what looked
to be a human interest story of value. But it was like
looking for a full-blooded Irish Setter at the city's
Humane Society's pound.

"And I wonder if you can tell me anything about
the Larry Curtland murder."

Father Wolfe stared at him. The reporter looked
like something out of the 1930s—except for his lack of
a porkpie hat. His hair was very short and he was
wearing large steel-rimmed glasses and jug ears—they
looked like add-ons, an afterthought of his Creator—
and was apparently very nervous. Was this his first
assignment?

"Sir, my name is Cyber Nettick." Another bizarre
name? Will he tell me his boss has another unlikely
name? Like Randy Jokes? The young man—how old
was he?—twenty-three?—twenty-four?—produced a
very official-looking identity card complete with his
picture. And there it was: *Cyber Nettick.*

"How did you end up with such a with-it name?"

Cyber blushed, looked down. He was embarrassed,
apparently, by his embarrassment more than anything
else. "My parents named me Simon. But I thought the
Si part of it would be better twenty-first century as
Cyber.

"Randolph Jokes"— *Are we in the middle of a sci-
fi fantasy?*—"he, the City Editor, my boss, thought
there was a good story here."

"I don't suppose you ever call your boss *Randy*, do
you?"

"Randy Jokes? No, sir." Not the flicker of a smile.
"We are always very formal in the office."

Is it possible he just doesn't listen?

"You know, why would a boy kill his father"—it was as though the priest had said nothing—"just for trying to help women who are in trouble?" *Doesn't this guy know where I as a Catholic priest stand on all this killing?*

"Didn't you get all the ins and outs of this abortion business when you were here at Kino as a student?"

"Oh, but I've been introduced to the real world since then." He looked down—was he blushing again?—as though he had just confessed to having won a bubble gum-popping contest.

"Did you talk to Larry Curtland?"

"They won't let me see him."

"Did you talk to the police?"

"They all say, 'Later.'"

"Well, I can't help you find out anything more about Larry Curtland. But I can tell you that I am on the other team." There was suddenly a loud clamor in the stands, and Father Luke looked over into the court where Barry Bentley lay on the floor at the center ring and watched the net embrace the ball. "Murdering a mother's baby is a strange way of helping a woman who is, as you put it, in trouble." A huge roar from the stands above him almost drowned out his words. "Taking a human life is murder, and I am puzzled that your paper doesn't want to investigate *that*."

"A potential baby, I suppose." He seemed to be rote quoting from *his* bible—whatever it was called. "But nothing more right now than a few vagrant cells."

"Vagrant cells? Potential? What are they the potential for, then, a peanut butter sandwich, an elephant, a stalk of celery? Does life mean so little to you that you wish your mother had disposed of you

91

when you were just a couple of *vagrant cells*? Are you that unhappy with life—with its glorious sunsets and Starbuck's coffee and young love?"

Suddenly Father Luke felt like a bully as the young man murmured something like *thank you* and seemed to have evaporated when he looked up. Had he been too pharisaical? He should have, he felt, drawn the young man out—socratically, just like in the classroom—and let him see for himself how logically he was wrong. Would he never learn?

Kino was still ahead. And they were into the fourth quarter. Whistle. Well, Jason Fitz from third period was at the free-throw line.

But as the ball arced up and in and the stands loudly approved, Father Luke was back at St. Luke's with *his* free throws to make.

On the one-and-one he had dropped the first one right through the center of the hoop—it probably had never touched the rim. And then the big one. The gym had been filling up with the crowd for the varsity game. And they were clamoring for a record. "Hundred. Hundred." Father Luke laughed at the memory. He knew he had to make this shot. He had imagined his putting it right through the center again while he bent over and bounce-bounce-bounce bounced the ball on the floor in front of him. As he stood up to make the shot, the stands had gone tomb-silent.

And then he had lofted the basketball over the backboard.

There was a continued silence of only two stunned seconds before the whole gym had erupted in laughter. He had choked. But his teammates had thought this was choice. High-point man for the night by over thirty points. Highest ever number of points in a single game for a player. And then he blows the chance for immortality. Choked. No century.

And there it was again. The gnawing somehow behind his heart. Had he passed his prime in teaching? Was Coach Sloan right? Yes, yes, of course, he was. The times they were-a-changing. But right enough for him to give up teaching?

That had been the last chance to prove himself on the basketball court. Only two games later he had tripped trying to out-fake the quick Emmonds guard and so badly broken his ankle that he never could run up and down the court for any length of time again.

TWENTY-THREE

"It was good of you to come on such short notice, Father." Mrs. Curtland was offering him a cup of coffee in what looked to him like Nieman Marcus porcelain—if Nieman Marcus made porcelain. Did they? "Sugar? Cream?"

Father Wolfe had done his prefecting chore at the Jayvee game. He would have stayed for part of the varsity game, just to watch three of his seniors. But he had promised Mrs. Curtland. And so he had collected car keys—#5 again—and quickly driven north on Kennedy, over to the freeway on Northside, up I76 to Swardley and out to 57th Street. The house seemed large enough to accommodate the whole Jesuit community and was set back far enough from the street to give it the elegance of a castle on the Rhine. *Money* was what the multi-mullioned windows spelled out to the world they regarded.

Mrs. Curtland had answered the door when he rang, and escorted him into a parlor he was almost afraid to look at, much less sit down in, so exquisitely was each piece of furniture and fixture just right. Suddenly like the sharp pain that had stabbed his left hip when he climbed the two steps to the front door, he wished he knew something about furniture. Obviously the curls and the curvings shouted *elegance* and *auction* and *antique* and *money*. But even to his unpracticed eye, they were simply accommodations that you must be very very careful not to spill your coffee on.

"Black. Thank you."

Tonight she looked the bereaved wife—rather than the cool and detached woman who had visited his classroom. Perhaps it was the indirect lighting. Perhaps it was the pale pallor of the wall of this room. Perhaps it was something she had done with her makeup. But now she looked lost, like a fawn in an empty field in a raging storm. A weak woman who had lost her husband to violence. Whose son was still in jail. But she was handsome still. But for all the looks of weakness very much in control.

"I hope you like it. Starbuck's. Larry said you couldn't abide the school coffee."

"It *is* a little hard on the stomach. It—the teachers' lounge coffee stands too long. Until it's acid." Father Wolfe took an exploratory sip. "Delicious. No, Starbuck's is not on our menu."

"I asked you to join us, Father—Oh, there you are, Arthur. Come and introduce yourself to Father." A young man slipped through the arcadia doors. He was maybe two years older than Larry, but otherwise could have passed for his twin. He was just as wide across the shoulders. And his eyes too were green, but of a darker hue. And he was blond like his mother. But there was a limpness and a reticence about him that was not Larry's. And he was taller.

"Arthur didn't go to Kino, Father, because he didn't feel he was ready for your kind of academic challenge." She smiled first at him and then at the priest. Somehow there was a joke here he didn't catch. All he understood was what seemed like a needless put-down. "He's going to Arizona State right now. And doing very well in computer programming. Aren't you, Arthur?"

95

Arthur nodded. There seemed nothing more for her to say about Arthur.

"Today I suddenly realized that in my grief I had come to cry on your shoulder in the wrong place—outside your classroom. I'm not going to cry on your shoulder now. In fact, I want you to know that I find it difficult to weep at all. Although I know I should. For Peter. And Larry."

Why was she telling him this? There was no need. This wasn't a confessional. Nor was this matter for the confessional.

"I am of course crushed by what happened to Peter." Of course. No commas. "I told you that. Catholic upbringing. And then the temptation. And the first abortion that changed him so completely. I understand now why we have confession, Father. And I have never known him to have gone since that tragic day."

There was something wrong. Why couldn't he put his finger on it? It was not in the way she was dressed. She was Arizona casual—jeans and a sweatshirt—of such dimension that at first glance it would have been difficult to assign its wearer's gender. But this reiterated, cold confronting of a stranger, even if he was a priest, with this poor dead man's wretchedness—what was wrong? Her husband. She had, after all, said, "I do. Forever."

"More coffee, Father?" She looked him full in the eyes and held him—as though they shared a secret. Did they? It was as though she had come over and knelt next to him, lightly finger-and-thumbing his shirt front, her eyes locked on his. As though she were trying to seduce him. Into doing what? But she still sat across the room. And when she looked at him there was nothing in her eyes. Nothing.

"No. No. This is just fine." He found himself sitting on the edge of the couch she had waved him to. And at the same time he found himself trying to back away from her. But without moving a muscle. And he wondered why she was not talking about her Larry. *Was all this cover for something? Had she initiated divorce proceedings? Was she having an affair? How to explain this detachment?*

"You aren't eating your cookies. Is there something wrong with them?" It was the quintessence of the matron's voice. The old fashioned totally-in-control schoolmarm.

He looked down to discover he had two toll-house cookies on the saucer in front of him. "No, they're just fine." And he smiled weakly.

Cool. Was that the word for her? Yes, in the current sense of *cool*—detached, above it all. And yet quite collected but un-warm. Uninterested. Was she involved with someone who had killed Peter? Did she know who killed Peter? Did she know if Peter had really been killed or had just suffered a heart attack?

"But what I really wanted to tell you, Father—I could hardly say it before your students—was that we—" She paused as her right hand went to her forehead as though to straighten a wig—"Arthur and I—want you to do everything—everything you can for Larry. I don't know what that is. But please do it." Was she going to cry? At last? Keep a stiff upper lip?

"I don't know what I can do, Mrs. Curtland. But, yes, I—"

"Did you enjoy your coffee, Father?" No, she was not going to cry.

"Delicious."

"I knew you wouldn't notice it. Nothing lethal. But one of Peter's *herbs*. You will probably have a twinge of nausea in a hour or two. But nothing like the amount I was tempted, so often, to give freedom to my Peter."

Freedom? My Peter?

"Freedom from all that evil, those murders, the killing, the— And the means was precisely the little hobby Peter had of collecting lethal herbs. That he with great satisfaction explained to me every time he found a new one. One that would never show up in any kind of laboratory as poison.

"Just so you would understand how I feel, Father." She smiled that cool smile again. So. This was the why of her invitation to visit. To make him experience the poison possibilities. But why?

Was everyone trying to kill him? Or bribe him? "Mrs. Curtland—"

"And you know, Father, I think I would have freed Peter with a little something in his coffee the very morning Larry did the deed."

But Larry hadn't done the deed.

"I felt sorry for him."

"Sorry? For Larry?" Luke seemed incapable of forming a rational question.

"For Peter. Somewhere he had picked up a flea. Or it looked more like fleas—in the plural. He was so covered with bites that morning that I just couldn't hurt him."

"Hurt him?"

"The pain of dying, Father. I still love him. Isn't that obvious?"

Not really, Mrs. Curtland. Not really. Should he come out and say just that?

"Did you, Mrs. Curtland?"

"Did I what, Father?"

"Did you add something to his coffee the morning he died. Something that would take several hours to work. Something forensics would never be able to trace, it was so exotic?"

There was a pause. She looked into the fireplace and at the modest flame that was quietly devouring the oh-so-thin stream of gas. Her right hand brushed her temple. "I wish I had. Oh, I wish I had." And like her son before her in talking about the actual act of killing, somehow she looked too small for the clothes she wore.

The thin line of her lips puckered. "Arthur, take Father down to the game room and show him Daddy's toys." She looked directly at neither Arthur nor Father Luke.

Still another contestant. Had this butterfly-fragile and lovely woman upstaged all the other wannabe killers? Was Peter Curtland's murderer sitting in front of Father Luke?

Father Luke stood up to follow Arthur. She now stood looking at him as though it were *the* scene from *Casablanca*. With those blue-mirror eyes. What were they saying?

TWENTY-FOUR

"He used to call that his Clint Eastwood. And this—" Arthur's voice was soft and pedantic, like a docent showing a tourist around an old, empty monastery.

"Why?" Father Wolfe was put off balance by the arsenal that faced him. There were rifles. And automatic weapons of some kind. AK-47s? M-16s? Most with labels. And revolvers. An old-fashioned Al Capone-looking Tommy gun. And pistols. Some tiny. Some large. Three of them silver-plated. Most blue-grey. He read labels where they stood clear. None of it was familiar territory.

"Did you see *Unforgiven*?"

"No."

"Well, anyway, that was the kind of Colt .45 Eastwood used in that movie. Long, long barrel." Arthur fondled the long barrel. His hands and arms seemed to belong to someone else. "Big gun. The barrel seemed half as long as a rifle's."

"There's another one just like it."

"Yes. Dad"—it was soft and quiet and sad, the first time anyone had talked to him about Dr. Peter Curtland with what seemed like any kind of real affection—"loved to remind us that when I was on the cross country team in seventh and eighth grade at St. Anastasius he got very much involved. He was so enthusiastic." Arthur smiled softly. And slowly. And seemed to take a large step backwards from his glasses. "He would not only attend every meet. He loved to start the race. But he wanted none of that starter pistol business. He had to use one of these long barrels. Dramatic. And he made up his own blanks, with lots of extra powder so that the big bang and the black cloud would bring a lot of attention. Sounded like a cannon."

"Quite a showman."

"That's my dad." Somehow he seemed unable to grasp the fact that he was gone, never to return to this display of killing tools.

"See, here's his work bench. That little gizmo is the machine he made his own bullets on." He smiled and did the withdrawing trick behind the glasses again.

"I really longed to stop him from being a butcher. In any way I could." He snuffled and rubbed his nose with the back of his hand. When Father Wolfe looked up, he was surprised to find tears welling up in Arthur's eyes.

"Did you try?"

"I talked to him sometimes when we were looking at his *artillery* as he liked to call all this." He made half a motion with his right arm to the guns. Diffidently. "But he always changed the subject."

"You tried to talk to him out of killing the children?"

"But when he didn't want to talk, I wondered if there wasn't another way of persuading him." Another would-be killer? How many were there? How many would there be?

"So one day I took this stun gun." Arthur gently opened the large drawer underneath the gun rack and brought out the strange-looking weapon. Like something from *Star Wars*. "And I went down to his office." Arthur's speech was getting slower and slower. "I would shoot him with it. Maybe it would shock him into realizing that it *could* have been a real gun. And that it *could* have killed him. And he might realize what he was doing to those babies."

Not the paint game gun Mrs. Smedana had insisted she saw in Arthur's hands.

"And you did it on the day that—"

"And I realized that with his weak heart the shock might kill him. And I decided to do it anyway."

"When?"

"Just as my father was entering the room where Larry was waiting for him and just before Larry went boom boom boom."

TWENTY-FIVE

Dear Chollie,

Look, I really need your help right now. Tell the Holy Spirit I am lost.

None of this Curtland business makes any sense at all. Everybody wanted to murder this guy. Well, not everybody. But Larry obviously didn't do it. And I didn't have the courage to draw Arthur's attention this evening—he seems to be a little slow upstairs—to the fact that there were all sorts of bullets in half-filled boxes there in his father's armory. I know nothing about guns, but I could read the boxes. And many were for .45s. And several boxes were blanks. Obvious. Larry in his panic and haste loaded up with the blanks his father had on hand for the track meets. Purposely? In haste? In his desire to kill the killer, but not really the man who gave him life? When I see him tomorrow, I will ask him about that. Dunno if it will help any. But I wonder why no one else has thought of that. Or have they just not bothered to mention it to me? The police must have known. Are they keeping things from me, just using me?

But that's only a mote in the afternoon sunshine: who did kill Peter Curtland? And why?

It doesn't seem to be Arthur. I thought he was going to tell me that he shocked his Father into a heart attack. But even though he took the stun gun down to his father's office and even though he was actually in the room when Larry opened up with the blanks, Arthur never did shoot his gun. At least, that's what he says. And somehow I believe him.

Deep down within me I wonder if I gotta come up with the answer to that big question loud and clear if Larry is to find his way out of his personal labyrinth.

Luke

TWENTY-SIX

"Hey, Father, did you hear?"

There must be some causal connection: whenever I open my classroom door before school, Tony Santos appears out of nowhere.

It was seven-thirty. Wednesday. Father Wolfe had squirreled his worn briefcase into the crook of his left arm and was turning the key to his classroom door.

"Heard what, Ton?"

Tears. When he turned to look at Tony, he could see the boy's face was awash with tears, sluicing down his cheeks.

"Rita's sister. Rita Poulos' little sister. Angelina. Last night. Yesterday evening. In their front yard. This car full of gorillas goes roaring by." He paused to gasp for air. "She's playing with their little spaniel. Jinky, that's what they called him. And maybe this guy in the back seat doesn't like spaniels or something. But he lets go with a bunch of shots. Bam. Bam. Bam." Tony's arm was outstretched to his left and his finger crooked over and pulled the imaginary trigger three, four times. "And one of the bullets killed Angelina instantly. In the back of her head. She was there playing. And she was gone. That cute little kid."

"Aw." And the tears started up in Father Luke's eyes as he dropped his books and keys on the floor of the classroom and grabbed Tony by the arm. "No."

Jesus, hug this little girl to Yourself. Right now.

"Did you know Angelina, Father?"

"No, Ton."

"They got the guy. Right away. A cop was driving slowly down the street. Just cruising. The other way. I mean he was coming at them. It was just over there. Half a mile from here. Like, nine o'clock. And the driver of the guy with the artillery gets so excited he takes off and slams his old Caddy right into the patrol car. The four guys in the car start to scatter but not before the cop tells them to hold it or they will be seriously ventilated—just like on TV. The killer's name is Joe Canty. And he's down in the slammer. The same one where they're holding Larry. Would you like to go over to the Poulos' with me after school? I'm sure Mrs. Poulos and Rita would appreciate it, Father."

"Sure, Ton. Glad to. If that will help anything."

"Mr. Poulos. He died just before Christmas. Huge heart attack, Rita says."

TWENTY-SEVEN

Chimes over the public address. Bing. Bong. Bing. Bing. "Please stand for the morning prayer. Einstein said, 'Creativity is more important than intelligence.' Lord, make us all creative in your service. We ask this through Jesus Christ. St. Ignatius of Loyola..."

"Pray for us," the class of seniors chanted.

"And pray for Angelina Poulos. And pray for her mother and sister."

"Who's Angelina Poulos, Father?" That must have been Andy Hall back by the book displays.

"The little girl five blocks over there"—Father Luke gestured generally northeast—"who was killed in that stupid drive-by shooting yesterday. Pray for them." *How little can we appreciate something that is not part of our lives. How can Andy—or I—even begin to appreciate the shredding that goes on in others. But we have to try. Or our prayer to You is no good, Jesus.*

"Einstein. Creativity. Well, I hope God gives you intelligence as well, guys." Father Wolfe walked from the doorway where he had been standing to his desk and his computer. "Are we all here today?"

As he passed Greg Farrell's desk, he stopped. "Greg," in that voice that only the boy would hear with all the other talk around him, "you could make your father *much* happier if you would do just a little something to justify your presence in this class and your father's fifty-five hundred green ones every year. Just a little something." He smiled. Like Santa Claus. "And he says he really *really* wants you to matriculate at Harvard."

Greg smiled in return. It was engaging. Even on the face that had lost its little-boy cheeks and now embraced the shape of a V that made it seem almost cadaverous. At first that smile split his face like Mickey Mouse's. And then it swept around you and embraced you. His brown puppy-dog eyes, somewhat enlarged by his black-framed glasses, lit up, and he was obviously your friend. For ever. It was a surprising addition to his lank, almost gaunt frame. And his casually mussed brown hair. As Father Wolfe gazed down at him in his desk, his mind conjured up the father's physique: one member of the family he did *not* take after was his father. Of course, not. He was *not* Dr. Brandt's son. Again that frisson of fear: was Sloan right? Was his memory still good enough for all of this?

"Sure. Right on." Greg brushed his hand through his not quite curly hair. "Tomorrow. Tomorrow I'll have this week's essay for you, Father. What was it on, again?" And again the smile—open, candid, you're-my-friend-forever.

"Pete." He punched his neighbor's arm. "What's tomorrow's essay about?"

"A short story, dude." Pete looked up at Father Luke—his eyes showed the irony of telling Greg again the assignment he had no intention of completing. "Like the *Hamlet* we have read so far. A parody, hunh, Father?"

"Greg. You have been promising me your assignment every week since the beginning of the semester now. And you have produced exactly none. Zip. Zippo. Zero for, let's see, six. Right? Why don't you start with this one? And do the rest of the essays

108

for the semester. And then we can all clap at graduation when you really do graduate instead of getting a diploma-aborted envelope."

"Yay. Cool." Greg happily joined in the fun.

"And." Luke floated the word up and down on his larynx like a carnival huckster. "You might actually learn something."

"Sarcasm. Father. Shame." Greg's eyes laughed as his mouth turned down. "No sarcasm. Please." He pushed his glasses up higher on his nose.

"You're right. No sarcasm. Sorry." And Father knew, of course, that as usual when he came around to pick up the essays, Greg would turn on that great smile and produce a waterproof excuse. And a new one and clever. Like, his little brother had spilled his cereal all over it just before the power went out on their block—even though he had no siblings. Or his mother when dusting had knocked the printer off the desk and it had refused to respond when he had just exactly enough time to print his masterpiece before he had to rush to school.

Father Luke went to his desk and, looking around the room, started to key in the absentees, realized he had forgotten to type in his password, had forgotten the password itself, caught himself as he was about to look toward the open door to see if Father Sloan was looking at him from the hallway door—was he getting paranoid?—dug into the back of the desk drawer, looked at a piece of paper stuck to its very end, typed the password and keyed in the two who were absent: Saalendranj and Garces.

TWENTY-EIGHT

"Well, Father, this may be a little disagreeable, I am sorry to say." Somehow Father Luke could not digest that "sorry to say." It just wouldn't go down—like a pill that was caught in your throat before the freeing gulp of water. Gerald P. Sloan, Father Gerald P. Sloan, always seemed happy with unhappiness. He had a long torso and as a result dominated his own desk from on high. And whoever was on the other side. And his curly brush of hair became a kind of crown, luxuriant and ever-so-neat, to enhance the regal appearance.

Whenever Luke saw Gerald Sloan so ensconced behind his desk, his memory automatically flipped back the pages to that day when he had asked the Gerry Sloan of thirty-five year ago, was it? who sat high torso-ed in the student desk what it was Chaucer was getting at as they explicated the description of the Monk in the *Prologue to the Canterbury Tales*.

Gerry had seen clearly enough that when Chaucer said the Monk was a manly man and worthy to be an abbot that this man would have made it anywhere: in the business world, in court, in law, in medicine. But when he got to the lines

His bridle, when he rode, a man might hear
Jingling in a whistling wind as clear,
Aye, and as loud as does the chapel bell,
Where my lord Monk was Prior of the cell...,
Gerry closed up.

"Gerry, what do the lines say about Chaucer's initial statement about the Monk?"

"That he had a beautiful bridle, whatever that is."
Why was Gerry bridling at this?

"Peter"—Peter D'Agostino had sat way back in the corner and was probably asleep: 10:30 seemed to be his usual daily nap time—"what's a bridle?"

A brief hiatus of silence. "That's—umm—the thingey the horse champs his teeth on."

"No, Father"—this from Sean Conner who sat immediately behind Gerry, Sean who could never wait to enlighten everyone from his vantage point of encyclopedic knowledge. "That's the bit. The bridle is the"—he paused just slightly—"thingey that holds the bit. The reins are attached to that. On both sides. And the *reins*"—he turned around and looked at D'Agostino and his voice took on the tone of mentor in an insane asylum talking to a drooling patient—"are the *thingeys* that you hang onto to steer the horse with."

"Thank you, Sean. It's amazing how soon the children of the Old West can forget some simple things their grandparents knew like the back of their hands.

"And so, Gerry, what was so special about that bridle?"

"It was a nice one."

"How nice?"

"Very nice."

"Was it expensive?

"Yes, probably."

"What was it made of?"

"Silver."

"Was that expensive?"

"I guess so." Gerry scarcely moved. He seemed to be scarcely breathing. His voice sounded as though he would lose himself if he said too much.

"Why would the Monk use something expensive to decorate a horse?"

"For the same reason you'd buy a Cadillac instead of an Escort, I suppose."

"To tell others he was rich?"

"Sure."

"Excellent. Now, what does that have to do with a Monk hearing a chapel bell?"

"Well, he should have been listening to it at the monastery to call him to prayer in the chapel." His eyes never once left the text in front of him.

"Terrific. Should the Monk have been out there on the road or back at the monastery at prayer?"

"At prayer."

"And with his vow of poverty, even if it was OK for him to be out there on the pilgrimage, should he have been driving a Lexus."

"No."

"Now what does all this add up to? What does the juxtaposition of the Chaucer's 'He was...worthy to be an abbot' and 'His bridle...as loud...as...chapel bell... do?'"

Sean was wriggling in his desk. "Irony, Father. Huge irony."

"Sean, leave this to Gerry."

"Irony." Gerry looked dazed. Clearly he saw no irony here.

Had he been too insistent? Father Luke reflected on his tone of voice. Had his voice had a sarcastic edge? Would Jesus have gone about ferreting the truth that way? He had scarcely ever concerned himself with such self-doubt when he was younger.

And the positions were now reversed.

Anna Wingold had phoned at the end of second period to remind him that he had an appointment with the principal in his coming prep period. Anna was still the pleasantest person around after having been the secretary through five changes of principals in ten years.

"Adrian"—Adrian Waters was in charge of academics, one of the assistant principals—"states in his report here that you have been dilatory in returning assignments to the students, students have found you forgetful of their names, and class never gets under way for at least fifteen minutes." After each member of the triad, his eyes lifted from the reading ovals of his bifocals and looked straight out at Father Wolfe. Like laser pointers. Only pale gray.

"He has brought this to your attention in several of his chats with you." *Chats* was Father Sloan's word for sometimes in-your-face meetings. Meetings that invariably found only fault. But never praise. Not even a crumb of support. Although the dictionary would probably defend *chats* somewhat differently.

"Under which tree?"

"Tree?"

"You know. Susanna. And Daniel. That was the question Daniel asked the lecherous elders."

"I wish you would be more serious, Father."

"Well, I am saying that Adrian told me that he was displeased, but he had no record of such accusations. Or conversations? Or when, say, I forgot a name? Do you have these in your file there?"

113

Novelists would describe Gerald's look as blank. No more laser. Blankly he stared at Luke—as though he missed the irony here. "Father, I wonder if you shouldn't ask Father Provincial to transfer you to another apostolate."

"Gerry,"—having had someone in class no matter how far back allowed of a breezy informality—"I find it wondrous strange that neither you nor Adrian has read the student evaluations of this old priest that is right now talking. Many were enthusiastic about the way I teach. Some were unhappy that I pushed them so hard." *Am I pushing too hard right now, biting too close to the quick? And some, of course, were just unhappy.* "But most were pleased that they were learning. A fair number even said that I was the best teacher of *any* subject they had ever had. That's a subjective judgment, of course. But are we talking about the same person? Me?"

"Anyone can be a popular teacher. Why don't we pursue this in our next month's chat? Meanwhile I will ask Adrian to"—he cleaned his teeth under his upper lip with his tongue—"be more specific." Laser eyes— but very wide open, to the distant blue of a cloudless day on a drowsy summer day—again.

"Gerry, you and I are Jesuits. That means that I will do anything Father Provincial wants. I vowed that to God fifty-and-then-some years ago. You talk to him—the Provincial, that is, Joe Sanders. Let me talk to him. I love teaching. You know that. And with all my faults you *know* that I am a helluva lot better teacher than many others here. But if Father Provincial wants me gone, I'm gone. But from where I sit right now, this is all unreal."

Father Sloan sat quietly looking at the report in front of him. He stroked the beard that was not there and dragged his chin down just enough to caricature deep thought.

"Why don't you visit my class? Any time. You haven't watched me in action since you were there as a senior. Thirty-some years ago. Forty. And why don't you talk to my students? There are better ways of finding out how well your teachers are doing than sitting here reading reports." Well, he shouldn't have said *that*. Not at all politic. Was that reflection honest?

Father Wolfe waited a moment for the "Case dismissed" and the sharp crack of the gavel. Neither came. "Thank you, Father" was all that walked with Father Sloan's wintry smile.

TWENTY-NINE

"And *why* must you have a comma after *friends*, Peter? Why? Why? Why?"

It was sophomores and third period. And Father Luke was dancing a little and poking his finger at this student and that and trying his best to stir up a little interest in punctuation.

"Is it because it's an introductory adverb clause?" Al Navarez offered his best smile as a chaser.

"Where's the verb? I see *My friends*. No verb. To have an introductory clause we have to have, Colin"— Colin was on the other side of the room, behind Father—"a...?"

"Verb, Father."

"And where, oh where, is the verb in *My Friends*? Tim?" Tim sat next to Colin.

"There is none, Father."

"And therefore, Al—?"

"There's a lady at the door, Father."

"No, Peter. We are concerned about the sentence in front of us."

"But there *is* a lady at the door, Father." Peter Dooling puffed out a little at having come up with a certain and unquestionably correct comment. Were ladies at the door going to become a *de rigueur* part of his sophomore classes?

Father Luke turned to face the doorway. There certainly was a lady at the door. There was a lady *in* the doorway. She was large. She somehow filled the whole doorway, right up to the lintel. She must have been six foot six or seven. She wore such an enormous bust that anyone who saw her was immediately reminded of the forecastle of an old sailing ship leaning out over you. Feisty. And when the priest got to the doorway he was able to see her face. He caught the gasp as it rose from within him. It was a mirror image of Michelangelo's *Pietà* Madonna—he had stood and contemplated it for hours on a school student culture-immersion trip twenty years before. Ethereally beautiful, innocent, little-girl young.

"Are you Father Wolfe?" The words were gruff and sounded as though she were calling him back from playing with his feral eponymous fellows out there on the desert.

"Ma'am, we are having class right now."

"I know damn well you're having class right now. But I have to see Father Wolfe. Right now." Mimicking him. Intimidating. In your face. Too quickly. "Are you that priest that's been seeing the Curtland killer?"

"Well, what's the emergency?"

The whole class was into this like a Nintendo game.

"My name is Ms. Lyda Lott. Roving reporter from Channel KNOT. You may have found yourself in the know by watching our gripping news show." Rote. Monotone. Rhyming. *Is she kidding?*

"What was your name again?"

"Lyda Lott." *This can't be for real.* And off to her right, there appeared a huge video camera, supported by a woman half the size of Ms. Lott. *A lot smaller.* It was aimed at Father Wolfe's face. They had been reviewing the prior week's test. He still had it in his hand, and now he raised the paper to screen his face.

"Well, are you?"

117

"I have seen Lawrence Curtland at the jail."

"KNOT's viewers would like a few words from you, Father, about this young man. Me, I am delighted that he done"—Father Luke's margin for surprise was diminishing, rapidly—"the deed. I wish I had taken that klutz out myself. He botched an abortion on me two years ago, and I have had nothing but hemorrhaging and infection and pain ever since. Even a quick brush with the Grim Reaper himself." She smiled a little smile that seemed to say she had personally faced up to that infamous character and done him in once and for all. "And if I had had the chance, I would have popped a thin"—she lengthened the word as though she somehow enjoyed its reluctant vibration—"wire around his throat and stretched it tight. I would have pulled it tight. Tight, do you hear? That half-baked, two-bit Lego mechanic." She seemed to be choosing her words carefully so that they could be aired while they covered for the bleep-worthy words she was thinking. (Was such thesaurus-work native to woman?) Her beautiful face moved even closer to Father Luke. Six inches. Truculent. Pistols at twenty paces. "Or jammed a plastic bag over his handsome pate." *Where had she picked up* that *word?* She did it now with her hands, forcefully, definitively, over the imagined head in front of her. And enthusiastically in great detail mimed the tying of a very secure cord around the bag around the victim's neck.

"Did you?"

Ms. Lott suddenly deflated. The following wind had ceased and left her sails like drying clothes on a clothesline on an airless afternoon—lifeless. "Did I what?" She stared at the priest. "Oh." A puff filled the sails again. "No. But I wish I had. I wish I had. He had it coming to him. Filthy amateur." The camerawoman was dodging back and forth. "Tell us all about our hero, Father."

"Well—" He looked straight into her eyes, smiled a quiet smile and tenderly stroked the white wisps across his scalp with his free hand. "I'm afraid I have nothing"—he turned his hands into inverted wings, the test paper still firmly held in his left hand—"to say, Ms.—uh—Lyda Lott." He had forgotten the camera and now brought the paper back up in front of his face again. "From that point of view." He smiled.

"Hey, Father, why dontcha ask the TV lady to take our picture?"

Suddenly Lyda and her *doppelganger* were gone. Like a wisp of smoke. Back to KNOTland. "Well, Jason"—Jason Carberry asked questions about everything: the walking, breathing antithesis of an encyclopedia—"I guess I just didn't think of it." Was he too caught up in himself? Had he handled the situation properly? Was this what Sloan was worried about?

THIRTY

The Poulos family lived in a neat brick house on Bartlett, four blocks north of Kino Prep and on the same side of Kennedy just a block and a half east. Twenty-six hundred square feet, maybe, and garnished with a fifty-foot pine on the left side of the front yard and enough bougainvilleas, hibiscus and Mexican bird of paradise to keep the place alive with color. And around the front door the ground cover of pansies and primroses smiled at the visitors as happily as toddlers when they hear the siren-song of the ice cream truck.

Mrs. Poulos sat on a couch facing the door looking like an old shirt thrown carelessly across the back of a chair. She had the face of a beagle, nicely humanized and with ears of more realistic length. And now crushed in on itself.

"Mrs. Poulos, I'm sorry." What else do you say? The clichés? Angelina must be with God? Was she? To say you *hoped* she was with God because no one knows another's disposition before that unknowable— out and beyond anything human intelligence can muster—Being seemed to belie the mercy of that loving Father. "Jesus is—"

"Father, they gotta put that beast away forever." And suddenly her whole body is stiff and hard. And her voice seems to be a ventriloquist's trick, coming from anyplace else but her. "I mean forever. Right now. With a hot seat. Or a forever arsenic shot. Or a noose over the nearest tree limb."

And all the while tears are niagara-ing, and she's ruining one tissue after another over her eyes. And her whole body is as tight as Jack Nicholson's smile when you should have picked up on his acidulous joke. "Angelina." And she has collapsed again, ready to be blown away by a passing breeze. "Oh. Oh." Her sobs come wrenched from deep in her subterranean self. Pain oozes from her like pus from an infected wound. "My lovely little girl." It's an unending tape. Except for the occasional indictment of the killer. "Bloody beast." She had settled deep into the far end of the single couch in the room as though she had become a part of it.

During all of this Rita is sitting on the same worn couch. She's crying too. And making the facial tissue manufacturers happy.

"Mom, you can't say that. Yes, Angelina's dead." Her voice is low and soothing a baby. "She's so good she's gotta be with God. But the guy that did this, Jesus wants us to forgive him."

"Forgive him?" Suddenly there was present a starting-up Indianapolis 500 engine with its straight pipes. "How can I?" She made the effort to sit up straight. "Forgive him?" It was more shout—roar— than anything else.

"That's what Jesus is all about. Forgiving. No matter the crime. You know that. He says it over and over."

"Murder? Murder of the innocent? My little baby?"

"He says He wants us to give ourselves away to everyone just as His Father does. And He did. On the cross."

Tony is standing there with his big square jaw hanging down. Staring at Rita.

Father Wolfe was mute, constricted. *Am I really hearing this from a teenager? Out of the mouths of little children—*

"It's so hard." The *so* tore at the walls of the room. How can God ask this of me? No. No. No. No. No." Mrs. Poulos was suddenly on her feet, swaying, staring at her daughter from three feet, lashing at her with her eyes. Her whole body was a bundle of bursting pain.

Rita looks up at Tony and Father Wolfe as if they will understand Jesus' joke and says, "Because He loves you, Mamma. He wants you right there with Him. At His crucifixion. Naked, spittle-covered, rejected crucifixion."

Well, *that* blew the clichés out of the water.

THIRTY-ONE

"You missed it, Luke. You were on the five o'clock news. Well, you were *almost* on the five o'clock news." This was Jack Philips. And it was supper in the Jesuit community. And Philips was at his owlish best. And he was addressing himself to his soup—split pea with a nodding acquaintance with a hambone—with the same precision and thoroughness that he employed to present a demonstration in his physics class. *The* physics class. The physics class for which, he occasionally reminded his fellow Jesuits as well as his students, he had been awarded the Outstanding Teacher of the Year award by the City of Phoenix for the last three consecutive years. And the same Jack Philips who was endlessly generous in doing anything that would help any of the kids in particular and the school in general. He had spent a whole month of twelve-hour days helping Father Luke install the shelves and programming the computers to go on them and then networking them all together with their printer and the internet in the old priest's classroom.

"Tell me about it."

"Well, you were there. But we certainly couldn't see much of you. A piece of paper kept somehow floating in the way." He winked at Bill Blazer, who was sitting next to Luke. "It almost looked as though you didn't want to be interviewed. Gee, all that great publicity for the school, Bill." Bill was the school President and was now staring into his bowl of soup clearly unhappy with "all that great publicity."

Jack laughed. It was surprisingly high on the scale and light for a man with such a deep voice. But it was pleasant, if slightly ironical.

"Luke, what *is* going on with—" There was sudden and boisterous laughter from the table by the window—Gerry Atkins, probably, with one his hilarious stories, told and retold—as funny, the way Gerry told it, the last time you heard it as the first. "—that Curtland murder?" That came from Louis Brown, the Rector of the community who fascinated the seniors with his Catholic Commitment classes, was a fussy-looking little man with the face of a cherub—rubicund cheeks and all—that belied his sixty-four years. It manifested the gentleness of a happy grandmother and cloaked what everyone who talked to him for even just a few minutes knew was the intelligence of a Thomas Aquinas—clear, sharp-edged, methodical, deep, satisfying, but always gentle and friendly. He stopped his methodical spooning of soup and looked up at Luke.

"I wish I knew, Lou. What everyone seems to know is that Larry Curtland continues to insist that he wanted to kill his father and that he killed his father and that if he had to do it all over again he would kill his father and—although he has mentioned no specific names—he would like to kill any and all abortionists. And that's why Judge Patterson refuses to let him out on bond—or any other way—even though the police are completely agreed that it is physically impossible for him to have killed his father." He took a deep breath. "At least with the gun he had in his hand when they apprehended him."

The Rector again paused in his metronomic offering of soup to his mouth. "How so?"

"It's pretty obvious. The gun was loaded with starter blanks."

"What kind of sense does that make?" It was Jack Philips again.

"None. None at all." *What more could he say?*

"Well, who *did* kill him, then?"

"I don't know, Al"—it had been the youngest priest in the community, Albert Friedls—into computers in his math class like a fresh coat of fire-engine red on a '73 Plymouth Roadrunner—who had asked the question. He wore a neatly trimmed Van Dyke that made his boyish face look surprisingly even younger. "The police are certainly not telling me everything they know. But I do know"—and everyone at the table stopped eating and looked at Luke—"that just about everybody I have met that has anything to do with the good doctor wishes that he or she had"—he paused—"'done the deed.'" *And so many could have.*

THIRTY-TWO

Father Luke drove to the south entrance gate of Kino from the school's south parking lot, and when traffic cleared, straight across Kennedy west into Longtree. The last of the day's light still hung out in the sky in front of him, and a mockingbird who had seen the underside of a joke seemed to be doing a Cactus Wren gig. You could tell it wasn't a Cactus Wren because the happy chirping came over and over again. And too quickly. A quick visit to Larry at the jail was the plan.

One hundred yards down Longtree, parked in front of the vacant single-story house that just last year had housed the ACE Taxi office sat a squat Humvee. Like a horror movie sewer supercockroach. It was desert dust—anonymous beige—in color. And Father Wolfe slowed slightly to get a better look at it. He had been fascinated ever since the Gulf War that people would buy such ugly trucks. And for a weighty bundle of Presidents' portraits on funny green pieces of expensive paper.

He drove by, looked at his fuel gauge, saw it was threatening drought, turned north instead of south on Third Avenue—numbered Avenues in Phoenix were to the west of Kennedy, Streets to the east—crossed Cartwheel Boulevard, turned right on Clarke and then back across Kennedy again and into the Chevron station where the school had an account.

As he left the automatic nozzle to fill the tank on its own, he washed the windshield. Reaching across to squeegee the far side of the window, he had the eerie sensation that he was being watched. Of course. Billy

Eckstein was probably the cashier tonight. What was that, the class of two years back?

But when he went in to sign for the fourteen gallons—he really had been close to empty—Billy was not there. And a quiet, heavily tattooed, balding man gave him his receipt.

As he waited to turn left—south—on Kennedy, he noticed a Humvee—it looked like the same one he had seen on Longtree—parked on the other side of Kennedy on Clarke, facing him. Spontaneously he spun the wheel right and drove north into the outside lane on Kennedy. He was being silly. Spooked. Who would want to follow him? This Curtland thing had him paranoid.

He took his foot off the accelerator as he approached the red light on Desert Flower. And in his rearview mirror he could see that the Humvee had made a left across Kennedy and was now heading north. With a quick look to the left to make sure there was no traffic, he suddenly turned left into Staghorn, gunned it—bright lights ablaze—to First Avenue, turned north again, turned off his lights on this side street and at a nervous thirty drove across Desert Flower and turned right on Mesquite and then back across Kennedy—the traffic had cleared as though they knew he was coming. He turned his headlights on again as he turned south on Third Street.

No headlights in his rearview mirrors. No cars, vehicles of any kind as far north as he could see up Third Street.

He settled back into the seat cushion. And he realized that his hand on the wheel was shaking. Well, that wasn't Parkinson's. That was his silly-old-man, stupid, unwarranted fear.

He crossed Cartwheel and turned right on Saguaro, the street just north of Kino, turned south on Kennedy, past Longtree to Dortland. He turned right on Dortland and then south on Third Avenue. That was complicated enough to shake any follower, real or imagined.

With a start he realized his mistake. He had forgotten that Third Avenue here was still north of the irrigation canal and he would have to take Brodrick either east to Kennedy or west to Seventh Avenue.

And suddenly he heard the mechanical growl. He looked into the mirror. And—was it only a yard behind him?—the Humvee—lights off—was on him.

Instinctively he floored it. With surprising catlike subtlety he touched the brake, spun the wheel to induce a skid when he came to Brodrick adjacent to the canal. Momentarily he was back in Reno the winter before he got his drivers license when his father methodically all through the cold and wet season schooled him in icy empty parking lots and country roads in the gentle art of handling a car in any situation—even the most treacherous slides and skids—to make sure that he would become one with whatever vehicle he drove and that he could always drive with all the skill of a stockcar racer. He would be off and away to Seventh, and the clumsy Humvee would not be able to make the turn.

But he was too late. As he started to spin, the insect eyes were on top of him. And right there at the bicycle path bridge over the canal, the giant truck with a sudden growl like a jet engine in takeoff slammed into the Neon's right rear and popped it up and onto the curb toward the bicycle/pedestrian bridge. The three-inch pipe, three feet high with its No Motor Vehicles sign, cleaved the front of the Neon like the waters of the Red Sea and set off the air bag. Up over the bridge and into the second post he was propelled. This time the seatbelt kept him from the windshield but not the steering wheel. Free. He had experienced the oddest sensation of freedom from everything—as though nothing could hold him down. Until he met what felt like a brick wall at ninety miles an hour. He had come to a halt on the other side of the canal, halfway into the return of Third Avenue. He was somehow aware that the Humvee was too wide to get across the bridge, and had dropped the right front wheel over the edge of the canal. But with a roar like a frustrated lion, the whole vehicle jerked back into the street and headed off toward Seventh Avenue. Would they cross there and come back to smash him again? This time from the south?

What was happening? Father Wolfe reached for his cell phone. Where was it? With difficulty—the Neon seemed to be lying on its side, the side opposite to him—he freed it from his pocket as he dangled in the safety belt. After two tries with fingers as jittery as the Parkinson's disease he was expecting any day but did not yet have, he managed to dial 911.

"I need the police. Car wrecked. Here at Third Avenue and the south side of the $75,000 bridge over the irrigation canal." Why had he added the starkly irrelevant price he had read in the paper when they were building it two years ago? "Between Havasu and Brodrick. It looks as though someone was trying to kill me."

He began to dial the school number. To tell Father Lou or whomever he could raise he would need someone to get him back home. And there in front of him were the cheerful headlights of a large white Chevrolet with the two-foot double vertical bumpers and the friendly blue and red roof lights laughing at him.

"Father Wolfe. We had better get you out of there if we can. Do you feel OK?" It was Perry Middleton. That had to be six-eight years ago. Middle seat in the third row on the windows side of the room.

"Yes, I think so. I was just signaling my engine room to do just that."

Perry gave him a mother-understands-everything smile. And started working at the seatbelt latch.

With the roar of that lion now cheated of its prey, a dust-brown Humvee pulled around the corner fifty yards down Third Avenue. It stopped suddenly and backed up and around the corner. But not before Father Wolfe saw a glint of something familiar behind the windshield on the left side. And he was suddenly aware that he had seen that same glint—the only single detail to identify the Humvee—just before it had caromed into him.

"Perry"—he was surprised that he could remember his name so facilely—"that's the guy who slammed into me on the other side of that bridge and knocked me all the way over here."

Officer Middleton on the instant was on his radio broadcasting an alert—Father Wolfe caught the words "Humvee" and "detain"—for his aggressor. And then Perry was back and helped Father Wolfe clamber stiffly out of the Neon. He carefully looked at each of his feet and then his hands: he seemed to be all together, although some of the pieces no longer seemed be very securely tied on. Another patrol car pulled into Third and turned on its red and blues.

"Feel good enough to tell us what happened, Father?" Perry's voice was a mother's talking to a sick child. "Fill out the report and all?" He had his notebook out and a pen in his capable right hand. He filled in the blanks and lines in response to Father Luke's explanation of all that he knew about the bizarrerie. He finally snapped the pad shut.

"Can we get you back to Kino, Father."

"Well, I was headed for the jail downtown."

"Oh, yes, the Curtland boy. Tell you what. Officer Rounds will be happy to take you down there. OK?"

Father Lou, a steady rock of complete concern, was suddenly beside him. "Do you feel up to it?"

The great advantage of living in community, Lord. There's always someone there and ready to pick up after you in need.

"Yes, I think so."

"Go for it. I have this covered."

THIRTY-THREE

Father Wolfe sat in the lawyer room chair and watched Sergeant Duchesne march down the corridor to bring Larry from his cell. Communion. His now daily visit was to bring Larry the Lord Jesus, mainly. What else was there to talk about?—they had marched back and forth over the parade ground of their arguments so often.

And again his mind arced back to Janey Peer. Why?

He was standing at the bottom of the stairs up to her front door. He had taken the Taraval streetcar down to the Mission District, got off at Fourteenth Street and walked up the hill to her place. She and her parents had moved out of the Sunset and down to the Mission in her freshman year.

He had been a little surprised when Janey had told him that she left for school at seven—when St. Ursula's was only two blocks from her house—and didn't start until 8:20. And when she had come out of her house and walked down the twenty-five—he had counted them while he waited—stairs, he was there to greet her surprised smile with his happy grin he somehow almost always found on his face when he was with her.

"Luke." It was somehow a question.

"Just thought I would walk you to school on my way to St. Luke's."

"Oh. That's nice of you, Luke." She turned to him and smiled that smile that always left him ready to burst with peace. Or was it joy? Was this what happiness was? Or was it what he himself was all about? "But I'm not going to school right away."

"That's why you leave so early." It was a question, really.

They had stopped at the corner of her block. It was a cloudless morning in September, one of those days that forgot all of the San Francisco fog and made you feel good about living in the most beautiful possible city in the world. And now she gestured to the right. "I go to Mass at St. Philip's every morning. Do you want to come with me?" She smiled at the question.

That's how it started. And by November on one of those rare mornings when he couldn't meet her, he felt somehow cheated, with a *For Rent* sign on the vacant flat window of his spirit.

Over the months St. Philip's became a part of him. It was old: it had survived the 1906 quake with not so much as a crack in a wall or a distracted statue of a Saint. Painted statues. All over. With enough vigil lights flickering to light the whole church, it seemed, without the bother of those Thomas Alva Edison things. The high, groined ceiling that loomed above and suggested higher things had darkened over the years, but hadn't weakened in its message. Behind the altar the high reredos with the statue of St. Philip on the left and St. Bartholomew on the right with the massive cross with the bloody Jesus stood in reverent awe over the tabernacle in the center at the back of the altar.

Although he had simply wanted to be with his Janey, it wasn't long before he found himself praying at these Masses, and reflecting on the priest's sermon words, and the Gospel. And Luke and Janey often talked about the morning's words of God as they walked the now only three blocks to St. Ursula's.

"I could see this coming a long time ago, Luke." On that last evening together, it was her answer to his telling her of his plans to enter the seminary the next day. "Each day at Mass I have prayed and prayed that you would find yourself. There. In Him. In the Lord Jesus. Together with me."

He never had seen Janey Peer again. The next morning he had left early to catch the Judah streetcar to the downtown commuter train station and then the train south down the peninsula and then the bus to the Jesuit seminary. Some years later he had met Sister Petronilla, who had somehow become much older and, although her order had eschewed any formal habit, still wore a blue veil with the density of a hymenopteron's wing. She had tried to keep up with the St. Augustine alumni, she had said, and had heard only the vaguest of rumors about Janey Peer. Janey had gone east to college, and then shortly after that her parents had moved away—no one seemed to know where. And then there was the disquieting story that put Janey into the rescue of two little kids in a burning car on a freeway country road up in New Hampshire or Maine. Janey—if it *was* Janey Peer—had saved the kids but died in the effort. She had a special talent for giving herself to others.

But he had often felt her quiet presence at his side. Especially at Mass. And was aware as he was now of the power of this woman in his life.

"Hi, Father Luke."

The two had prayed, Larry had received His God, they had talked for a while.

THIRTY-FOUR

Dear Chollie,

What a day this has been!

Gerry called me in. Wants me to quit teaching. And I was belligerent in telling him somewhat impolitely to get lost. Shouldn't have done that: Ignatius wanted us to obey even the subordinate officials. Should have been polite and kindly and Christlike. But deep down I wonder if he isn't right. Am I riding on my own self-esteem? Am I doing any good at all? Would a younger man do better? Most of the time I feel that he has the bat by the wrong end. Inigo—why did he ever change his name to Ignatius? Inigo of Loyola seemed just fine for our number-one Jesuit—was right on in focusing on Jesus' insistence that riches is the noose that drags us into defiance of God. And my feeling of at-homeness in the classroom is a riches. And there are times like right now when I think I am a fool to buck Gerry. That he is right. Chollie, tell the Spirit to come to help this old guy. I'm still having so much fun in that classroom, trying to trick the kids into grasping a little logic about their language. And their lives. And Jesus.

And then there was that TV news reporter. She came. I saw. I know not if anyone conquered. I just had nothing to tell her. Not that I wanted to. But the police have kept me in the dark. Cliché. They are happy to use me to help them find the killer. But to me it's the third monkey with his hands over his mouth.

After school I went with Tony Santos to visit the Poulos family. And that was something.

I hate wakes and funerals. Because you're supposed to say the right thing. And particularly because you're a priest you've gotta say the right thing. And the "right thing" is the wrong thing to say. The really right thing to say is that we hope and pray that the deceased is rejoicing in the full rich vision of the ineffable God. And ineffable of course means that we don't know what we're talking about. We do not know what that person's dispositions were before God. We hope. But that's not the right thing to say. We've gotta say that the departed is with God. And after that, what is there, really, to say accept that you're sorry and what were the final circumstances and all the other banal comments we make in the face of shock and ignorance? Because it's not our grief. And it's only a metaphor that makes it ours. Unless you're deep into the reality of the Mystical Body of Christ yourself and can make that pellucidly clear.

But this was different. Mrs. Poulos was crushed. For all her deep love of God evinced in her militant demonstrations against abortion, she was not only completely unhinged by her loss but completely caught up in playing God's avenging angel. Fire and brimstone, too. Mt. Baker revisited. Popocatapetl squared.

But her daughter Rita stole a march on her outraged spirit. She has her hand in Jesus' and speaks Him from His heart. And hers. Tony said it on the way back: "She's really something, hunh, Father?" She is.

THIRTY-FIVE

And then the accident. Well, let's call it an accident, anyway.

Somebody or somebodies just about killed me on that little bicycle bridge over on Third and the canal. Totaled our Neon. Got a ride to the jail.

Talked to Larry. Nothing has really changed. He's getting itchy. But nothing else is really different. Every time I go down there the very bleakness of the jail makes me wonder why he doesn't blithely promise them anything just to spring free. I know. I know. "Stone walls do not a prison make, / Nor iron bars a cage..." But somehow this just doesn't fit Larry—except for his simple candor.

"Don't you want out of here?"

"Of course, Father."

"Don't you see that it's just plain wrong to kill another human being?"

"Nothing is changed, Father. Of course. Unless you are bashing with a baseball bat the guy who is smashing others with his baseball bat." His smile is back. The funny smile that simply stretches his mouth pencil-line thin across his whole face. The one he had featured daily in the classroom. Open. Sunny. That just barely showed the lips of a nice clean, white row of teeth. Like a little kid's. Yet hyper-aware of all that is going on.

My heart goes out to him. But I cannot budge him. Chollie, lean on the Spirit to turn this kid around.

On the way out, Amy Duchesne shook her red halo just once as she paraphrased a paper on her desk. "Bunch of kids high on something. Crack? Ecstasy? We don't know what yet. Stole the Humvee from Burger Hamm"—she looked up at me to see if I knew he was the Scorpions Hockey Team's owner, and when I nodded, went on—"and decided to have some fun with the first 'little' car they could find."

"Do I know any of them?"

Their names meant nothing to me. And that glint I thought might have been Doctor Brandt—well, so much for hasty conclusions. A stray bit of light reflected off the rear-view mirror, I guess. But who else has even the remotest reason for killing me? That threat of his was obviously just plain old macho bravado. There was no one else with them when the police picked them up.

Luke

THIRTY-SIX

"Mary, teach us to serve your Son with gusto."

The class chanted a boisterous "Amen."

The class of seniors settled into their desks. "That was very good, George." George was boxy and stiff like a Snickers bar standing on end—with the sweet personality to go with it—, and it was George Appleton's day to introduce the brief prayer to Our Lady after the *Hail Mary* to begin the class. "Did you come up with that all by yourself? It sounds like a beer commercial."

"Well, that *is* where I got the idea, Father. But it's still a good idea, isn't it?" George smiled his economical, wooden—if kindly—smile.

"Shouldn't he have said something like 'We would please like to ask you for the gift to serve your Son with gusto,' Father?" Tiny Troy Wintergreen's sharp voice floated in from the back window corner of the room.

"Well, Troy." Father Luke straightened his straying hairs. "When Jesus taught us to pray in the *Our Father*, every line is imperative, straightforward, making it clear that in some wild way we are on a level with God himself."

"You priests always want to have the last word." Was it necessary to point out to Troy the irony of that comment?

Harry Smathers wanted to get in on the act. "Just Johnson absent today, Father."

"Isn't it just plain interesting that he seems to be absent every Thursday? Do you suppose it in any way coincides with the writing assignment due today?"

"Father. Sarcasm. No, sarcasm, remember?" This from Greg Farrell two rows over.

"Well, then unsarcastically let me put in my password, and you, Harry, can do the computer deed. If I can remember that password." But he could and punched it in, and after he got up, Smathers settled into the teacher's desk chair.

"For Monday, since we do not convene—umm— on the weekend, gentleman, I would like you to read the selection from Samuel Pepy's—that's pronounced Peeps—*Diary* that you will find on page 675 of your literature book."

"Father, somebody wrote in my book that it's pronounced Peepeez."

"You will find, Troy, that just as you have come to call Casa Grande Casa Grand"—Father Luke gave the first a heavy Spanish softness and the second a flat Tennessee twang—"so the Britishers had their way of personalizing their pronunciations. Byron's *Don Juan* immediately comes to mind. It looks like *Don Wan*. But the English say *Don Jew-wahn*. Peeps." He was surprised by the awareness that he was getting all this fun from being sanctimonious.

"Read it for Monday. And now I will pick up your *Hamlet* parody. And then we will continue on in reading *Hamlet* together."

The pattern was the usual one as Father Luke went from one student to another, picking up and glancing at each student's effort: the same ones who faithfully turned in their effort turned them in. And then there were the usual excuses. And the usual mute responses.

"Father, is Larry ever coming back?" It was quietly put.

141

"Looks grim, Al." Al Flyte was still Larry's best friend.

"Doesn't that old Judge Prenderville—"

"Patterson, Billy."

"—know that Lar couldn't hurt a fly. He's just too nice a guy."

"Just exactly what that judge doesn't know."

Father Luke came to Greg Farrell. And he started to continue on down the row to Jerry Garson. But Greg was handing him a sheaf of papers neatly stapled in the upper lefthand corner. Father Wolfe mugged a huge surprised look and took the papers. Glancing at them he saw immediately that it was all there, four pages: cover assignment and three pages of double-spaced narrative about a Kino student who was trying to decide whether to revenge himself on his buddy who had upstaged him on the soccer team.

"Will wonders never cease? What brought this on, Greg?"

Greg was at his affable best. He had what it took to take it all the way to 1600 Pennsylvania Avenue. That smile that opened up his face. His deep-sea blue eyes that sparkled in the recognition of the irony of a huge joke. "I fell in love, Father." He ran his hand through his already rumpled dark brown hair.

Next to him, Harry Connors laughed a fun-and-games laugh.

"Well, Greg, falling in love usually has the opposite result on academic activity. Time spent with the damsel torpedoes responsible study time. How do you explain—?"

"It's a paradox, Father." That was Harry again.

"Yes, it is. How *do* you explain that paradox, Greg?"

"Her name is Alice Grunch, Father." Harry Connors couldn't stay out of this.

"No, that's not her name, Father. Greg looked down at his hands folded on his desk. "But she is absolutely beautiful and completely good. And if I can have anything to do with her at all, I have to be somehow worthy of her. I have to be the best man that I can be." He looked up. His eyes were bright—was that the beginning of tears? He pushed the sagging glasses back up over his nose.

Harry was on the verge of a talk-show laugh. But suddenly even he realized this was for real.

"Marvelous, Greg. Now, shall I give the *A* for this paper to you or your inamorata?" Something stirred in Father Wolfe's mind, then broke into the clear: it wouldn't solve the murder of Peter Curtland.

But it could—might, Dear God! would—change the whole picture of Larry's incarceration.

THIRTY-SEVEN

"Tony, I want you to find Rita Poulos for me." The bell had rung. Students were nudging one another out the door and toward the next class. Luke had stood at the door of the classroom and had waited for Tony Santos to come by.

"Dunno if she's in school today. Like, funeral. And all."

"Does she come to Kino for any of her classes?"

"No, Father. I'll see if I can find her at Mother Teresa. Then what?"

"I need the two of you right after school for two hours."

"What gives, Father?"

"If you can find her, I'll tell the both of you at 2:20. Here. Right here."

As Father Wolfe turned back into the classroom, he found himself face to face with Doctor Brandt. The man seemed to appear out of nowhere.

"Father, I didn't mean to frighten you." He wore his bass-mouthed Peter Lorrie gentle smile. "I was on my way to the office, and I wondered if we have progressed in any way with regard to my son's graduation." Father Wolfe backed toward the door as Doctor Brandt moved closer. And there it was, the quick glint of light from the doctor's glasses. Suddenly Father Luke felt the urge to scratch his arm.

"Not yet, Doctor. But perhaps your son has. You might want to ask him about the whole situation yourself. Earlier this morning in class, a door opened wide for a change for the better. Why not talk to him yourself, Doctor?"

There came that unnerving flat laugh. But ever so polite. "Well, thank you, Father. I'll do just that." He smiled. And he was gone. Suddenly.

Was I too brusque with the good doctor? Jesus, give me Your patience. And help these two guys to get their act—acts—together.

THIRTY-EIGHT

"I guess I got you into all this, Lar."

Rita Poulos was sitting in the chair across from the desk. Would she be strong enough for this? She looked starkly frail in her Mother Teresa blue-plaid—they all knew now it was the Campbell clan's—skirt and white blouse. Captain Parsons was standing in the corner. Next to the door. Skeptical. Larry Curtland sat behind the desk across from her in the lawyer room at the Landor Jail. Tony Santos and Father Luke sat side by side next to the door in the north corner of the west wall.

"Not really, Rita." He looked at his fingers outspread on top of the desk in front of him. "You talked me into demonstrating. My father"—he paused; he sounded as though he needed more breath in his lungs to continue talking—"my father talked me into all this." He turned and looked directly into Father Wolfe's eyes for one long second.

Father Luke finally caught Captain Oscar's eye and with that look gently but clearly suggested the officer leave. With the slightest of nods and an uncharacteristic hunching of his shoulders The Law slipped out of the room.

"And of course, Father Luke had already laid down the ground rules for me. But he isn't responsible either. What I wanted to do is what had to be done. As I keep telling Father Luke, it was a pre-emptive strike: I paralyze you before you can destroy me."

It was a chance. A hope. A prayer.

Lord, please make this work.

Tony had, at Father Luke's request, picked up first Rita at Mother Teresa's—she had been excused from school for the rest of the week but had decided to go to class for two of her most difficult subjects—and then Father at Kino. It was difficult talking in the topless Jeep. They had bounced and buzzed past the skyscrapers and their walls of sightless eyes, which somehow looked a little less daunting in the sunshine. What was it Jesus had said about the light? But on the way down to Landor and Seventh, at stoplights and with a bit of soccer-field shouting in between, Father Wolfe had explained what he hoped for. Why he wanted them to talk to Larry Curtland.

Captain Parsons had ushered them into the lawyer room and gone for Larry.

As soon as Larry had entered the almond-walled brusque box, barren except for the desk Larry now sat behind and the three unfriendly chairs across from him—someone had added two metal folding chairs from somewhere—Rita had smiled. And suddenly Larry was smiling. And Tony and Father broke out into grins. Even Captain Parsons' lips twitched a little and his eyes softened.

What a beautiful girl she is! In spite of her pain. In spite of that nose. Or perhaps because of it. The whole place is alive with her joy. And in such a fragile vessel. Now, send her Your Spirit, Jesus, to do the job.

"Lar, ask Rita to tell you all about it." Tony touched the very center of his shaved head with the end of the fingers of his left hand and lifted his eyebrows. He had understood what Father Wolfe wanted him here for.

"About what, Rita?"

"Larry, something"—Tony sat forward in his chair and twisted his hands together before he opened them out in a gesture of candor—"terrible has happened."

"Larry, my little sister, Angelina, was shot by a drive-by killer. And she died a few minutes later in my mother's arms. 'Goodbye, Mamma. I think Jesus wants me now,' was the last thing she said. And smiled. And was gone." Rita looked straight across the table into Larry's eyes as the tears cascaded down from her own.

Larry stared back. Transfixed. "Rita—" His mouth remained open. But he seemed incapable of another word. Would Rita give him the whole story?

"Her killer's down here with you, Lar." Tony was right on cue. "Somewhere." He looked past Larry through the big window toward the cells. "They caught him right away. Did a stupid maneuver trying to disappear."

"Rita—" Larry seemed incapable of anything more. "You must really want to get that guy and—"

"That's the way my mother feels, Lar.

"And that's the way I feel too, Lar." She looked straight at him. "And every time I think about him, I want to vomit. And something deep down within me wants to tear him apart. And throw all the parts to some wild dog. I want to hate him and destroy him and stomp on him and rid the earth of even the vile stink of him." She suddenly seemed twice her size.

Larry was caught up in her vehemence across the desk. Tony was bundled up within himself, head protected by the hands he was holding it in down by his knees.

And just as suddenly as her tirade had all started, Rita seemed to collapse. "But I can't."

And then she smiled. The sun smile again. Warm. Warmer, surprisingly, through the tears. "I just can't square that with Jesus. He tells me over and over again to hate the crime." She half-sobbed. "And the crime stole Angelina."

She looked up and straight into Larry's eyes. "But he asked us to forgive the evil-doer. I want to hate him. But I can't. I can find peace only in praying for this poor guy who is so deranged that he would steal my little sister from us. Put him in the hands of the gentle Jesus to bring him to say 'I wish I hadn't done this awful thing.'"

Father Luke suddenly became aware that her face and the front of her blouse and handkerchief were soaked with her tears. And she seemed so small and suddenly frail again that Father Wolfe had to catch himself up. He was about to get up and take her in his arms and rock her like a baby. *Have I been too cruel to ask this of her?* But he knew he must not. It would spoil everything. And when he saw that she was silently sobbing, he found he could not see for the tears in his own eyes. He knew he must leave if she was to be free to work the magic he hoped for. Now. He reached for the doorknob next to him and slipped out.

John Becker, S.J.

THIRTY-NINE

"Can you tell me how it went?" They were parked next to the Kino Jesuit residence on the Kennedy side now. Father Luke had waited and waited outside the lawyer room door. But it was only fifteen minutes. Tony had opened the door; Father had motioned to Captain Parsons, who had taken Larry back to his cell.

On the drive back to Rita's house, it had been impossible to talk. And Tony and Father Luke had escorted Rita to her door. As she stepped inside, she turned and smiled. It was weak. But radiant and all there. What was to be said? "Thank you," was all Father Luke could think of as he looked deep into her eyes. And Tony and the priest had gone back to the Jeep almost as though they had left their souls there at her front door.

"I'm sure. And I'm not sure, Father. But something happened to Lar. But I don't know if it's what you wanted." With the engine off, it was suddenly very quiet. Even the steady distant clamor of the Kennedy traffic seemed somewhere on the other side of the globe. "Rita was, like, terrific."

Tony paused, looked off toward the passing Kennedy cars. And then turned back to the priest. "After she told him what she *felt* like doing to that creep who killed her sister, she told Lar how wrong it was. Not the feeling. That's just emotion. But her mind was telling her, she said, that it was all wrong. And it was all wrong because Jesus had told us to love one another. And not in just any old way, but the way He loved us.

150

"And Larry wants to know what that has to do with murderers. And he starts talking again about getting them before they get you.

"And when he's all done with the angry lecture, Rita says, 'Yes, Lar, but that's not the way He did it. He could have clobbered them all when they wanted to nail Him to the cross. And all He says is "Father, forgive them." And if Christianity means anything at all, that's what we gotta do. Forgive them. Not kill them. And Jesus knew that those same people that had destroyed Him were going to kill his Apostles. And He said, "Father, forgive them."'

"And then I hear Larry say, 'My God!' Kinda half shout. Half prayer. And I look over and he is staring at Rita. With his mouth open and out of joint, kind of.

"And Rita—I thought she was gonna collapse— says, 'And if I could, I would go into that jail cell where they have Joe Canty and I would give him a hug.' Her voice had become just a whisper. 'Right now. But not because I feel like it. I don't. I think Jesus would like me to kiss him, too. But I don't think I have the strength to make it feel genuine—after what he did. But I do want him to know—'she sobbed as though she could hardly breathe—'I want to love him—with Jesus' love.' She just stopped talking then. And looked like she was gonna cry a little more. But she was cried out. And sat there, washed out. But looking straight at Larry, with her lower lip dragging a little, like a little kid's.

"And that's when Larry gets up, in a kind of daze, and pushes his chair back and stumbles past the desk and over to Rita and kneels down in front of Rita and takes her hands and kisses them. And now *he's* crying.

"And Rita leans over and kisses Lar on the top of the head and in a strong whisper says, 'Larry, forgive your father.' And his head goes down on her knees. And he kind of goes limp, you know. And I wondered if he had fainted."

Tony looked off to the passing cars on Kennedy. "And that's when I came to get you and Captain Parsons."

"We have a bona fide living Saint in our midst. And her name is Rita." Somehow it seemed just a cliché—nowhere near the truth.

"If she isn't, Father, there's no such thing."

"Did I ask too much of her? In her pain?"

"Well, I think that's what did it, Father. After you left, it seemed like she let it all out, wasn't holding back or worried that it was you who should have been giving the sermon.

"And you saw for yourself how someplace else Larry was when Parsons led him back to his cell."

FORTY

"Father Wolfe, where is my son?"

Father Luke, looked at the glowing LED numbers on the alarm clock next to his bed. It offered an insouciant and redundant 3:33. In the morning. And Friday. Couldn't the world let him sleep? Well, at least couldn't Doctor Brandt let him sleep? He had recognized the voice immediately.

"This is Doctor George Brandt, Father." Yes, Luke did know that from the voice. And the assertive arrogance. "Where is my son Gregory Brandt?" Well, Gregory, anyway.

"I think you've come to the wrong person, Doctor. How should I know where your son is? I thought I was the bad guy on your block."

"You know very well that something has been happening to my son. And undoubtedly it has to do with his graduating. And his mark in your class. And that means that whatever is going on, *you* are responsible. Where is my son?"

"Well, Doctor, I suggest that you phone the police. The missing persons bureau."

"Such duplicity!" And Doctor Brandt was no longer on the phone.

Father Luke found himself absent-mindedly scratching his arm.

FORTY-ONE

Tony was there, almost *of course*, as he opened the classroom door. "Have you heard if it worked yet, Father."

"Not yet, Ton. Soon soon, I hope. I'll let you know just as soon as I know."

And there was Greg Farrell standing next to Tony. "Father, can I use one of your computers?"

"Sure, Greg."

"The library's closed, Father. I could see some guy messing with the carpet and stuff inside, and a big sign on the door said the place was closed for the day. And I gotta have this Catholic Commitment paper for Boris—uh, Mister Bofford—for first period."

"Feel free. Boot up #10, though: it has to come on first in the network—the tie to the printer. I think I left the server on. I thought you had the world's newest and most powerful cyber tool at home. Isn't that what you told me when you turned in your—ummm—first essay of the semester yesterday."

"I moved out yesterday, Father. I told my mom I was going to live with my Aunt Clarissa. You know, old maid aunt. She lives alone up there in the early numbers on Insouciant Lane. I know, I know: irony. Just one of those crazy Phoenix street names you like to play games with. Anyway, she used to take me to Mass when I was a tiny tot since she figured I needed some religion and my Catholic mother and my un-Catholic-ed father seemed to wanted none of it the way Aunt Clarissa understood it."

"Why?"

"Well, it's Teri again. The girl I told you about. Did I tell you that was her name—Teri—with one *r* and an *i?* She has forced all sorts of conclusions on me—just by being who she is. And what she is. She is sooo good." His big mouth opened, and his happy eyes rounded into a smile.

"Anyway, we were talking yesterday, and right out of nowhere I see clearly that to try to be honest the way she is honest means that I can no longer let the money my father makes by murder support me."

"Sounds like the women are wrapping us around their little fingers." Tony winked at Father Wolfe."

"Well, let's hope so, Ton. This kind of woman, anyway."

"And she lent me her '75 Pinto and said 'Welcome!' and I went over to Fearless Frank's—your hamburgers and subs and stuff—on Cornflower and he said he'd hire me at minimum for thirty hours a week. That will take care of gas and money for my food offering to Aunty."

"At this rate, you'll soon end up a Trappist monk."

"Um, don't count on it, Ton. Just yet." And the super-salesman smile turned on. "And hey, guys. Don't tell my father. Do not tell my male parent. Be sure—"

"Like, why not, man? He's gonna find out." Tony hunched his big shoulders.

"Sure. But I hafta work this thing out for myself. I don't want him jamming it down my throat. Father understands. I'm sure. OK, Father, Ton? So which one is #10? Hey, I bet it's this one over here by the window with a large number 10 on its monitor."

FORTY-TWO

"Father Wolfe? This is Captain Parsons."

"Yes, Captain." Instant silence tented the class as they concentrated to hear. Second period, and they had hardly opened their *Hamlet* after the memory recitation of the "When in disgrace with fortune and men's eyes—" sonnet, when the phone rang.

"Father, how soon can you get down here?"

"Where?"

"Well, uh, the jail—but not the jail." For just a moment Captain Parsons' composure disconnected. "Judge Patterson— Something happened this morning. And Judge Patterson wants to see you at the Main County Courtroom. In the basement of the jail on Jordan. At Third Avenue. Um—as soon as possible."

"Is Larry all right?"

"Oh, yes. Yes. That's not the problem."

"Problem?"

"I'll explain when you get here. You *will* come down, won't you?"

"I have class until 2:30. Three o'clock?"

The class stirred as soon as he hung up. "And you were going to tell us, weren't you, David, what was so ironic about Mel Gibson leaving out the last two lines of Act Three Scene Three?"

"Well, Father." David Soundtree always spoke as though his hearers already knew what he was saying and his information was patently obvious and stale news. "Like, Claudius—"

"Just plain old Claudius."

"Just plain old Claudius—" The class as one person snickered. "—is there praying. And he is asking

God to make him *want* to be sorry for his sins of lust and avarice. He had killed Hamlet Senior because he wanted to be king and he wanted the queen's body. And now he asks God to forgive him."

"What's so ironic about that?"

"Well, nothing." David paused to consider that. "Except that he knows he's gotta give up both the queen's body and the crown if he wants God to forgive him." He looked up like a little boy expecting a pat on the head.

"And?"

David frowned and looked back at the book. What had he left out? "Well, in comes Hamlet. Hamlet Junior, that is. And here is his chance to kill the killer. Nobody around to tell the tale. But he doesn't kill him."

"Why not? Because he's a ditherer? Because he can't make up his mind?"

"No. No. Hamlet wants revenge. Revenge squared. To the tenth power. He wants to get his uncle *better* than his uncle had killed his daddy. And so he decides to kill Claudius some other time. Not when he is praying. Because if he is praying when Hamlet murders him he will go to heaven. But if he can catch him sinning a big fat mortal sin and kill him then, well, he'll send him straight to hell." David pointed down to some locale subterranean and clearly miles below the classroom floor. "Yay! And that's worse than Claudius had done in sending his father to purgatory."

"Excellent, David. But what's so ironic about all that?"

"Well. After Hamlet leaves, Claudius gets up from his knees. And he is sad because his prayer was no

157

good: I mean he could not give up queen and crown. And so God couldn't forgive him."

"And?"

"Well, if Hamlet *had* killed him, then while he was still glued to his sins he would have gone straight to Satan's macrowave."

Bing. Bong. Bing. Bing.

"Excellent, David."

As Tony Santos walked past him to the door, Father Luke said, "Would you like to drive me downtown this afternoon, Ton? By this time in the day our Jesuit cars are probably all signed out. I think maybe—I hope—Rita did the deed."

FORTY-THREE

It was break.

"Father." Tony stood there at the door as he started to lock up on his way to the teachers' lounge for a gulp of acidulous coffee.

"Tony." He picked up the boy's eyes with his and laughed into them. And Tony laughed back.

"Father, Mrs. Poulos says the funeral for Angelina is tomorrow. At ten. At St. Emydius. Mrs. Poulos was going to ask you to say the Mass, but in talking to Father Harkin—"

"Yes. He's St. Emydius' pastor, Ton."

"—everything seemed to be settled, she said, before she even thought of bringing up your name."

"As it should be."

"I suppose most of the Mother Teresa girls will be there. Even though it is Saturday."

"You aren't planning to demonstrate at the clinic this week, then?"

"We're going over after the funeral and the cemetery, Father. Rita says there's no holiday from shouting to the world that murder is murder." He touched his bald head for a moment. "When are they going to bury Doctor Curtland?"

"I haven't heard. I suppose forensics want to keep on checking and double-checking the body."

FORTY-FOUR

Judge Wilfred Patterson looked up from the cigar he was trimming.

"Father Wolfe." He waved to a chair opposite him, but didn't get up. "Captain Parsons." And another grandiloquent gesture to the chair next to Father Wolfe.

"Sorry I had to get you down here, Father. Cigar? Father? Captain? No? I hope you don't mind if I smoke." He did not look up to see whether they did or not. The actual lighting was like a religious ceremony. Slow. Deliberate. Reverent.

"Let me explain. This morning Larry Curtland asked to see Captain Parsons. He said he wanted to talk to me: he had had a change of heart."

Father Wolfe could not suppress a smile. Something deep inside him relaxed.

Thank you, God!

He wished Tony could hear this, but Captain Parsons had insisted that he was to wait outside by the secretary's desk: only Father Wolfe was to see the judge.

The three of them were seated in Judge Patterson's oak-lined quarters that still faintly smelled of the lemony Endust whoever had cleaned the room had used that morning. The room was behind—south of—the judge's courtroom in the basement of the jail.

"As you know, Father, the reason I have remanded him to prison here, even though we are all convinced that he physically could not have killed his father as he said he had done, was that he publicly and loudly stated that the only way to get rid of the murderers of yet-to-be-born-babies is to kill the murderers. Which clearly put all abortionists in jeopardy. Even though he did not *state* that *he* was going to kill all abortion providers."

Wilfred Patterson looked the way he spoke. His large girth matched the large leather chair that girth embraced. And with his head aimed at his desk, he looked up to talk to Father Wolfe—like the clerk in Norman Rockwell's portrait of the couple come to get their marriage license: head down, to the side; eyes up and on the happy couple. Life and all living things were under scrutiny. And Judge Patterson was the skeptical judge.

"If the boy means this"—he waved the cigar and its smoke trailers to his right—"there is no reason why he should not be given his freedom." He took a heavy drag on his cigar. "But if this is just a hoax to get out of jail"—again he waved his cigar—"then he stays right here in the slammer." Hardly in character, such a word. If only Tony could hear this! Rita *had* pierced the crust of Larry's façade. "Do you understand what I am saying, Father?" He shifted his weight so that he was now sitting upright behind the desk and leaning forward.

"Yes, I do." Does he want to be called *Your Honor* or *Judge* or...? *Jesus, now is the time to send us Your Spirit!*

Wilfred Patterson fell back from the desk again and into the embrace of his chair. "Now, I am not of your faith, Father. I'm a Mormon. Mostly." He looked at the cigar in his hand like a diabetic staring at the offerings in a See's candy store showcase. "But I do respect what you people are trying to do. And I understand"—

at least someone still said understand—"that you have had a number of conversations with the boy. And that he likes you. Accordingly, do *you* think this is a ruse?"

Father Luke felt like gushing. Of course Larry meant what he said. Why had Rita come down to see him yesterday? Why had he wanted Rita to make sure Larry saw in *her* great pain that she had seen that killing and vengeance were no good? Why had she so gently told him that what Jesus had said was true? She knew it in her bones. And why had he felt that even when he could not convince the boy, the turnaround in Greg Brandt had shown him the power of a good woman on a man's heart? But he knew this was not the time to gush.

"Now, yesterday, Father"—came before Luke could say a syllable—"this girl Rita Pohloos—"

"Poulos."

"—Poolaws came to visit him. You were there. Do you think she effected a change in him?"

"I—"

"Do you see my predicament, Father? I want this boy out of here. But I cannot send him out into society a menace behind the business end of a gun." And he waved the cigar at the walls in general, at the whole world.

"What happens if I say I think he really means it?"

"Then I free him to his mother's care and remand him to your responsibility."

"So that if he kills someone I am responsible."

"Something like that." The smoke gentled up from his cigar held motionless in front of him in the silence. The judge looked up over his glasses and stared at Father Luke. "What do you say, Father?"

"I don't really see why you should doubt his word."

FORTY-FIVE

Chollie,

You were certainly leaning on the Lord, my friend.

Larry had little to say on the way back. What he did say was that Rita had blown him away. Forget all that logic about pre-emptive strikes, as due and proper in their place as they are. If you were a Christian you simply do not take a life. You could condemn the crime all you wanted, but you hadda forgive the criminal. And if you weren't a Christian—why worry about anybody else, whether they are helpless infants or your father? Suddenly it was all so very, very simple.

Judge Patterson had very solemnly asked him if he was sincere in his new attitude to abortionists. And when he said killing was no longer in his life, the judge explained to him how I was responsible for him. Somehow. I still do not really understand how I can be responsible for another human being. When he agreed to this, we left.

I was "fit to bust," as the old cliché went. But Ignatius would have said I was experiencing consolation. "...any increase of faith, hope, and charity and any interior joy that calls and attracts to heavenly things..." as that man said. Even when we got back to Kino and I said I would take him up Kennedy to home while Tony stopped on the way to his home to tell Rita the good news and find out the time of Angelina's funeral, I was standing tall, about nine feet high, when Larry asked me if I would get Father Gerry Atkins to hear his confession. What a surprise! I was surprised. And hurt. And back to five feet ten and half again. I had been working like crazy for him. And then he wants to put the whole wonderful denouement under somebody else's by-line. And then, of course, I realized that that was childish and stupid. The only important thing is that Larry find Jesus' peace. I had a good laugh at my pettiness. And could hear you laughing too, and lifting one of your bushy white eyebrows and then the other, as you always used to do when I did or said something foolish.

And then Larry was suddenly embarrassed. He said it would be cleaner and straighter to explain to God through a priest who didn't know him. I agreed.

FORTY-SIX

We went into the Jesuit residence together. When Father Atkins came down, he smiled his tired smile.

"I would like to go to confession, Father."

Pierre looked blankly at me. I nodded. "Well, let's go down to the parlor, then, young man."

As I sat waiting in that love seat—an abandoned and un-loved reject from some by-gone school auction—in the hallway outside the office of President William P. Blazer, S.J., you jumped into my thoughts. Ten years or so it was, you stayed up all night just to listen to me talk. Well, maybe not all night. But it must have been closer to four than to three when I finally quieted down and we headed up to our rooms and bed. Just to listen to me in my anger at the injustice—anger and I guess fear, too—that I just couldn't shake and needed to talk out.

I little realized as I waited out there for Larry and caught up in reverie how soon I would find strength by trying to emulate exactly the same kind of kindness I had found in you.

"You are gone, Father. Gone." That had been Benny Grouwl, the father of Al. Al was a very bright student. That was obvious: he loved to make apt comments in class. He wrote startlingly fresh essays and stories in and out of class. Even now I can see him quietly waving his hand in class and quietly voicing the

pertinent comment that pretty much finished discussion on the matter at hand.

But at the end of the first semester, my marking book read 20, 20, 15, 45, 37—those are percentages, Chollie—for his assigned book tests: he had clearly read none of the novels I had asked the class to read and then to prove they had read and then to critique. Al had received two progress reports promising a final D for the semester. I had personally handed him the tests with their bargain basement grades—as I always do for all tests for the students—with no comment from Al as he took the papers from me.

No, Al was no precursor paradigm for Greg Farrell. Greg had been doing nothing. Al was on top of the whole English scene except for reading the assigned books.

When Benny—head honcho at Benjamin J. Grouwl and Associates, "Bulldogs of Justice for Your Rights After Personal Injury"—saw that final D, his Stanford plans for Al disappeared down the drain. "You will never teach another class at Kino. You will never teach in any other school. Mark my words. And if Kino can survive what I'm suing you guys for, it will be a miracle that even St. Thomas More will bobble." I was surprised to find that Benny knew St. Thomas was the patron Saint of lawyers. Irony.

His voice had the steady, monotonous edge of the thoroughly angry and the thoroughly righteous and the thoroughly convinced of their own rectitude. "What happened? How can this be? Al has never, ever, in his whole life fielded a mark lower than an A on any report card. In anything. Ever."

Al claimed he had gotten a 90 or better—a flat 100 on two of them, Cry, the Beloved Country *and* The Lord of the Flies. *But he had "never kept the tests." And, he said, he had never received the progress reports.*

Progress reports that I forgot to insist that he return, signed by mother or father. We were now seeing the results of my forgetfulness.

And now Benny was going to sue the school—for two million bucks, at a time when we didn't know where we would find the money for the month's salaries for the lay teachers and staff.

Art Chase had been the Jesuit President and Principal all rolled into one at the time. He seemed very much inclined to believe Benny and Al rather than yours truly. I suppose it didn't help matters that up till then Benny had been a big contributor to the school. Irony.

The next day all was resolved when Scott Bord, the youngest lay teacher in the school and head of the English department, offered to question Al about the books in front of his father and me. And Al blew every last one of the questions—not just some or a few, but all— even though he had had of course ample time to prep himself on all of them.

Benny and Al never said another word about the matter.

Art apologized. Said he was sorry he had for even a moment left me in doubt.

It was you who kept me sane the night before the grilling that cleared the air. You listened as I let loose my frustration and anger. We were down there in the community room. And you simply sat there looking at me. Occasionally you lifted one of your wonderful eyebrows. You said next to nothing. But you were there. There. For me. You were your gift to me.

When Larry and Pierre came down the hall from the parlor, Pierre smiled first at Larry and then at me, waved a small wave with a slight hand gesture and slowly headed up the stairs to his room.

Larry smiled his thin smile as I stood up to leave. I had even started to push open the door.

"Father Luke." Larry paused and looked up into my eyes as I looked back at him. I was holding the door open. "It's soooo good to have it all right again."

And then it came. Huge male sobs. From deep deep down inside him. He reached out and grabbed me, burrowed his head in my chest and sobbed. "What a fool!" His voice was muffled. "Oh God, how stupid!" It was clearly a prayer. He seemed to be getting weaker and weaker. It was no longer a hug. He held me for support. "My own father. Daddy. You gave me life—me."

Larry dragged me back down to the couch with him. "And I tried to kill him. Wanted to kill him. Can God forgive that kind of evil?"

He wasn't talking to me anymore. But I had to fill in the void. "Yes, Lar, He's crazy about you."

There was a short pause. And then, "Oh." And then, like a sigh, "Thank you, Father." I'm not sure which father he was talking to—there were three possibilities, I figured. And then he did sigh, long and peacefully. He relaxed and pulled his legs halfway up onto the seat and up against his stomach—so much like a fetus that I was tempted to look to see if he was sucking his thumb. He lay there huddled against my side with my arm around him.

Then we sat there, motionless, for—I don't know how long—a half hour? Longer? An hour? More? And I found that you, Chollie, were somehow—although there really wasn't room for all three of us on that love seat— sitting there with me—us.

Finally, he seemed to become utterly quiet and calm. "Are you asleep?" Stupid question. "Shall I take you home now?

He stirred a little and came back from the edge of the universe, slowly, as though he were walking that infinite distance in bare feet over pebbly ground. Father, please take me to Grandma Curtland's instead."

Larry's hair was a mess, his face was blotched red and white as he looked into my eyes for understanding. "I'll stay there for a while. I've done it in the past. Grandma doesn't mind. I'll explain later. I don't want to talk about it now."

All of this was in a near-whisper. "She lives just a couple of blocks west on Cartwheel, and a block or two north." He was exhausted but deep into peace.

"Oh. And Father Atkins said I should tell you. You should not have brought me Communion—I was so committed to evil."

I must have turned all colors—me, with my disparaging comments about politicians who insist on receiving Communion when they endorse the murder of abortion.

"Well, maybe it wasn't such a bad mistake to make—you received the Lord and His power to get straightened out."

Larry smiled. "Yes.

"On the way can we stop at Rita's place so I can"—he paused and smiled—"confess to Rita?"

We did. And then Grandma—Mrs. Beatrice Curtland, widow of Dr. Alexis Curtland—welcomed him with the kind of hug only warm, loving, understanding and slightly overweight grandmas know how to effect.

We still do not know who murdered his father. But somehow I don't care much any more. It doesn't seem to impinge much on what was really going on.

Luke

John Becker, S.J.

FORTY-SEVEN

Father Harkins, Dil—his parents wanted him named Delbert after his maternal grandfather, but someone in the family could not spell—had asked Father Luke if he wanted to concelebrate. He had said no, he just wanted to stay in the back of St. Emydius with everyone else. Besides, he knew from past experience that Dil had a unique charisma. He was a priest's priest. When he said Mass he brought everyone in the church almost immediately to God's feet, aware that they were in the presence of the Being that was beyond their imagination—*ineffable* again was the word—to whom they owed everything they were, Who was just goofy about each one of them, individually, personally, for ever. Always. And today, anyway, Luke did not want in any way to fragment the focus of that awe-filled prayer.

Tony sat in the front left pew with the Poulos family. And Luke was here, in the back, amongst strangers, partially behind a massive, rotund pillar. He could see Dil clearly in white vestments beneath his unruly shock of crow-black hair with the high forehead warning of stark baldness soon. And he could hear him as well—the sound system at St. Emydius was magnificent. A pity, he distractedly thought, he could not steal it for their Kino chapel where he always had to strain to hear the speaker, no matter the voice timber.

He knew where the half-size coffin was—he had gone up before Mass began to bless it and hug Mrs. Poulos and Rita and Tony, and say nothing—but now he could not see it.

172

Dil had scarcely started on his homily. As usual he had caught the attention of everyone there. His words were ordinary enough. But it was Dil—like John the Baptist?—himself who hooked their minds. And held them. "...like the Jesus Who is the way and the truth and..."

In spite of Dil's power, Luke's mind was gone. Some-other-place City. He knew he was still there in the back of St. Emydius. But he was suddenly caught up, somehow in the word *truth*. Was that Dil's MO—to bring you into yourself before God Himself from whatever he had been saying?

But it wasn't the word itself. Nor was it truth as such. But he suddenly felt—knew and felt, experienced deep down somehow—that this whole Peter Curtland thing had to be resolved. No, not re-solved. It hadn't been. Just solved. Not because the murderer had to be brought to justice. That was a reason. But it was not *the* reason. And it wasn't somehow to clear the Church's reputation that She had now in many people's mind of fomenting the assassination of baby-killers. No, that wasn't it either.

On the surface it was easy: Larry Curtland was all right with God. And in a sense that was all that mattered. But there was something more here. Unless the real killer were recognized—who cared, in a sense, if he or she were ever or never apprehended?—Larry would forever carry this albatross around his neck. Luke knew this now with absolute clarity. And conviction.

And he was also aware that he, Father Luke Wolfe, must bring this truth about.

Or at least *try* to effect it.

173

He knew it in the very same way that he had known fifty-some years ago that he had to become what he now was. Bobby Hirt had insisted that they see *Citizen Kane* together. They had gone to the pricey Biloxi on Geary and 35th, and it was at the very end when *again* the sled was thrown into the furnace that he knew. He knew what the sled symbolized in the movie—*not* in all of its priapic imagery that he would find out about only years later. But the sled stood for Kane himself, for his very soul, for the innocence he had lost.

But he also suddenly and definitely and clearly saw that he must become a Jesuit priest. Where the intuition had sprung from, he had no idea. How had Janey known when he didn't even know himself?

It was like Sebastian in the *Brideshead Revisited* that he would read years later. Waugh had made it quite clear that this young man simply knew that he was and must be and could be nothing else other than a Catholic, even if his living that identity left more than a little to be desired. Such was simply part of his identity. Of his very essence. It was St. Ignatius' first way of making a valid choice as he expressed it in his *Spiritual Exercises*.

And now, like at the Biloxi, Luke experienced that same kind of awareness about what he must do for Larry.

And he did not know why. Now—a half-century-plus later. Or then. If you had asked him then why he must do this, he would have said something that was true but somewhat beside the point like: It's the best thing I can do with my life. Or the Jesuits will make me a great teacher. Or—

And ironically he had known no Jesuits. He had had no desire to go to their school. But then, there, he knew. Felt. Experienced.

And today in St. Emydius church, back behind the orotund pillar, he knew.

That day at and after *Citizen Kane* he had felt totally incapable of telling Bobby. Or, later, Janey.

He had never been able to make it clear to her. How he felt. Or why. And even today he wondered if he himself had really understood. Or did even now.

On the Saturday the letter had arrived from Father Provincial saying that he was accepted as a Jesuit novice, a trying on of that way of life with no commitments for two years, they had gone to St. George's parish dance. And afterwards over the casual hamburger and milkshake at Leo's Burger Pit, he had tried to tell her. How much he had longed for and looked forward to their *What a Wonderful Life!* I Do after college. That she was to keep his class ring. And his love for her would never change—and it never had—no matter the apparently alien course of his life now. He smiled at the irony. That evening he had felt wretched. And brutal. And at the same time could not allay this terrifying drive that was tearing him away from her—that he wished he could somehow avoid.

Janey had said next to nothing after that. And then he took her home. When he kissed her goodnight at the top of the twenty-five steps up to her front door, she cried a little. "I could see this coming a long time ago, Luke"—he heard them often in his mind's ear—"ever since we started going to Mass at St. Philip's together."

175

John Becker, S.J.

"Ever since we started to go to Mass together? But, Janey, I thought you loved me. All this time I thought you felt about me the way I felt about you."

"Oh, Luke." She smiled and ducked her head down a little. "I've loved you ever since fourth grade—when I noticed your crooked smile and funny ears."

"I knew they were big, but I never knew they were funny."

Then she looked straight at him and held him with her eyes for a long moment. "I love you. Always." She kissed him again. Strong. And tender. Then she smiled—that smile that threatened to pop his heart out of his chest and made him feel the great joy of being alive, now so alien to him in his devastated awareness that he would never experience it again—and turned and ran into the house.

And here today he saw no opening of light to solve this murder. But somehow that he had to do everything he could to open up this whole killing business to the bright and clean light of the sun. Had to. With that same insistence that tore him from Janey.

Jesus, where do I go from here? Send me Your Spirit. Send me Your Spirit.

FORTY-EIGHT

Chollie,

Help!

Where do I go from here? That's what I have been asking the Spirit.

I feel like one of those hamstrung soldiers in the old days of sword battle. I have to fight the good fight. But I find myself helpless. Like lying prone on the ground wanting to get up but unable to move my legs.

Where do I begin to solve this mystery? Forget the why. God seems to be insisting that I do what I can to free Larry from this monkey on his back.

And he is just one of the potential murderers.

This whole weekend this business has been sitting on my mind like uncooked bread dough in my stomach. Like a cancer. A tumor. When I said the 8:00 and 10:00 Masses at St. Benedict's in Three Pines, I pleaded with the Lord Jesus to give me light in all this. And all I could see was that nothing was solvable.

As soon as I began to retrace the whole situation, I realized that maybe Larry really had killed his father. Maybe the explosions and the pointed gun had done what others hoped they could do—produce a heart attack that would carry him off.

And that held for Mrs. Semantha. Maybe she did make it in time to scare him with that absurd costume.

177

Maybe Arthur neglected to tell the whole truth. Maybe his stun gun had stunned his father to death.

When I asked Parsons if there were any marks on Dr. Curtland's neck, he sadly said yes. Did our TV amazon garrote him as she said she so longed to do?

Forensics, Parsons tells me, found no evidence of any cause of death in Dr. Curtland. But from what Eudora Curtland had told me, precisely such poisons was what he had been cultivating. And she knew how to use.

Doctor Brandt had maybe played the same game with Doctor Peter that he had threatened with me. Or maybe as he bent over him ostensibly to check his pulse he then gave him the coup de grâce for whatever any of the others had provided the shock for.

The wife and sons wanted the world freed from a baby killer. Lyda Lott wanted revenge pure and simple. Well, not really very pure. Mrs. Smedana wanted rid of baby killers, but also wanted a twisted kind of vengeance for the seduction of her daughter and the murder of her grandchild.

And Brandt—like Semantha—had two motives if John Finney is on target. With Peter Curtland's death he would have the whole abortion abattoir—why don't we use that word in public instead of "clinic"?—revenue all to himself. And did he hope to have Peter's lovely wife all to himself?

And was that another motive for Eudora Curtland? Was she a party to Brandt's greed and lust?

See what I mean?

Chollie, I find myself totally incapable of correcting another paper. I tried. Yesterday and after I got back from Three Pines. But helplessly mulling over this Curtland thing has been my grand oeuvre of the weekend. And now I have nothing to return to the students tomorrow.

And I have gotten nowhere. And it did no good whatever to find Mr. Smedana's sagging cheeks and prognathic toothy smile at the switchboard to happily greet me with, "How's the priest-detective this lovely afternoon?" In fact, it called up like an acid stomach how tenuous a handle I have on all of this, no matter how clearly I see I must find an answer.

Chollie, HELP!

Would it help to take this matter up with the Little Lady Who Is Jesus' Mother? Why not? Women do have a way with them, don't they?

Amen.

Luke

179

FORTY-NINE

It was Monday, the second period of the day, seniors. Fourth period according to the rotating schedule. His sophomores in the prior period had been strangely quiet—even for a Monday. Not that he was complaining.

"Mary, teach us to tell Jesus yes as honestly as you did." That had to be Harry Watkins—the voice was a clearly articulated deep seemingly angry growl, ironically from a boy who was perennially happy about everything.

The class shouted, "Amen," and sat down all at once like a huge but graceful dromedary.

Father Wolfe picked up the pack of quizzes on his desk and handed one to Martinez and another to Szetczinich. He wanted it pronounced SET-n-itch. And as soon as he thought about that, Father Wolfe found himself scratching the itch in his arm again.

"Father, what's this?"

"Your 'Samuel Pepys' quiz. I asked you to read—"

"But, Father, don't you remember?" It was Szetczinich again.

"—his diary. The fire of London."

"You told us at the end of the class on Thursday that you were canceling that quiz so we could have the whole period to do our *Hamlet* presentations."

And so he had. He was suddenly aware of his forgetfulness and angry at his inability to keep such simple things as this where they belonged in his day. And it would be just fitting for Sloan at this very moment to take him up on his invitation to visit his class at any time—at any old time—to witness his mnemonic confusion.

"All right, guys." He felt suddenly very tired. "Who's on first?"

"What's on second?" That was Smathers. And he followed it with a barked laugh. Scattered laughter ruffled through the class.

Father Wolfe smiled. "Not bad, Harry, not bad at all. We'll have to give you the Smathers award for that. I meant Who goes first?"

"You told us—" It was diminutive and precise Barry Tang, sitting right beneath his elbow. "—that we'd have to draw straws. The producer/directors would all have to be prepared on the first day. And then you would draw straws. That's what you said, Father."

"So I did. Well"—Father Wolfe looked across the class—"who are the assigned producer/directors?"

Seven hands went up—three enthusiastically and four rather hesitantly.

Father Wolfe pulled out a pen from his left breast pocket and a card from his right, glanced at the card, turned it over, stepped outside the classroom to where he could not be seen by the class and wrote the number three on the other side. He came back in, holding the number away from the class and said, "Joe, number from one to ten?"

Joe hesitated. "Nine."

"Barry?" Barry looked around at the rest of the class. "Uh—four."

"Al."

"Fifteen?"

"Al"—Barry let his impatience show—"it's gotta be one to ten."

"Four."

"No. That's the number *I* picked."

"One."

The whole class relaxed a little.

"Larry?"

"Threeee." Big and bold and brassy. His eyes laughed as if he somehow knew he had drawn the right number. Father Wolfe should not have been a little surprised that Larry was back in class. But he somehow had not expected him. And he smiled his pleasure that the "old" Larry was the one who had returned.

Father Wolfe showed them the card. "That was it."

Laughter, nervous and scattered. Somebody said "Yeah" enthusiastically. And added, "OK. Hop to it."

Larry Curtland was into it immediately. He stood up, walked to the front of the classroom. "Look, guys, we gotta use the first row here. You first-row guys wanna move to the back someplace." It was a statement, not a question. Larry had taken over the class. "We need the front of the room for the stage and the first row for the people in the play who view the play within the play. That's the scene we're doing."

It had all started a week and half ago. Why hadn't he remembered it this morning? Each day, line by line they had worked through *Hamlet* until they were at the beginning of Act Five and had just started with the gravedigger give-and-take when Austin Drusc (Austin pronounced it DREE-sitch) had raised his hand and insisted, "Father, this is all very confusing."

"I know, Dree, but you're going to see the movie soon."

"But I'm lost *right now*."

"Me too." That was from a voice by the door, followed by scattered agreement across the class. Father Luke looked hard at each of the students around the room: they were clearly sincere. But before he could comment, the bell had rung.

And Father Luke had slept on it. And the next day he gave them a list of seven famous *Hamlet* scenes, with the number of characters involved in each. They were to sign up and choose their director from their number, memorizing the lines and coming prepared with some sort of costume to conjure up in the class's mind the personality of the character they were portraying. He hoped this kind of involvement would clear up the confusion in their minds.

"We're going to be doing the first part of the play within the play." It was Larry talking. He seemed to want everyone to be clear about what was going on. He had donned a large black sweater and a very blond wig. The front row desks had been moved to the front of the room and turned laterally so that the class could see the reactions of those seated in them. The "stage" itself was thus the area at the front of the room between the second row of desks that had now become the front row and the three desks facing each other on opposite sides of the classroom. The ones on the right were to the left of and next to Father Luke's teacher desk and computer.

FIFTY

"Just so you do not get confused, me, I am Hamlet. Of course." And Larry smiled his political candidate smile. "Father Wolfe, since you're standing right there at the door, would you be so kind as to turn off the lights to the back of the classroom to emphasize that the front up here is the stage." And when the lights had gone off and on again, "Thank you."

Joel Sweeters was gesturing to Father Wolfe from across the room. He motioned opening his window with a question mark all over his face. He then mimed choking. Father Wolfe had nodded and then opened the door behind him and quietly pushed it up against the hall wall. They did need a little more air.

"And I am going to be sitting over there in front of Ophelia"—there were snickers from the class: Larry had gestured at his friend, six-foot-four-inch potato-body Al Flyte, All-Phoenix High School Linebacker, who now wore a dainty girl's handkerchief on his head as the only indication that his regular school shorts and collared shirt gave him the *persona* of the delicate girl who was Hamlet's beloved. "Greg Ferrell there"—here, Larry turned to him and gave him a swoop of his hand—"is the Player King." Greg wore a Sacramento Kings cap that blazoned *Kings* and now had the *s* inked out.

"And Joe Balt"—who had found an enormous muu-muu someplace and had haphazardly gathered it at the waist of his six-foot-two, one hundred and twenty-pound frame—"is my mother Gertrude. Claudius the King"—somebody said "Boooo"—is played by Bert Kline. Bert had donned a cardboard

Burger King crown. "Harry Smathers"—as Harry stood up he turned first to one side and the other and then slowly in a complete circle to show that he was wearing a shirt that was black on the front with white letters insisting that *BLACK IS BEAUTIFUL* and white letters on the back with corresponding black letters that said *SO IS WHITE*—"is the Player Queen." Harry was wearing a Kino baseball cap backwards; an over-size deck of cards Queen was stuck into it and hung down over his forehead. "If you're wondering how the Player Queen could possibly be a black, well, we'll explain it to you if you come around humbly after class." Harry let go a huge guffaw that fought with the little-boy smile that followed.

"Now, we're going to truncate—Father Wolfe said it would be OK, remember?—the player king and queen lines. This way they will make more sense. Just as we did when we went over it in class. But we'll keep the famous"—he narrowed his eyes and looked askance at the class—"and naughty lines. Lights. Camera. Action."

Father Wolfe was still standing in the doorway. He flicked the switches—carefully to avoid the frog's noisy comment—to turn off the back two banks of fluorescents and leave lit only the set over the front of the classroom.

"But here and hence pursue me lasting strife, / If, once a widow, ever I be wife!"—Harry Smathers, who had donned his mother's slightly faded apron had started.

"If she should break it now!" Larry-Hamlet came in from the left front of the class, right on cue.

John Becker, S.J.

"'Tis deeply sworn. Sweet, leave me here awhile. / My spirits grow dull, and fain I would beguile / The tedious day with sleep." Greg Ferrell-Player King emitted a huge yawn, stretched generously and was lying on the floor before he had finished his lines, his glasses somewhat askew as he lay on his side.

"Sleep rock thy brain; / And never come mischance between us twain!" With that, Harry Smathers-Player Queen had tiptoed off the stage like a Count Dracula in drag.

"Madam, how do you like the play?" Larry-Hamlet turned to the muu-muued Joe Balt-Gertrude-Real Queen.

"The lady doth protest too much methinks." Joe delicately fluttered at his face with a fan he must have picked up from a Chinese restaurant.

"O! but she'll keep her word." Larry heavily emphasized the *she'll*.

"Have you heard the argument? Is there no offense in 't?" Bert Kline, who was sitting by the window next to Joe Balt, puffed a little as he said it and adjusted his paper crown to remind the audience that he was Claudius the King.

"Well, it looks as though I picked the wrong time." This was a whisper next to Father Wolfe's ear. He had not heard the footsteps come up to the open door behind him. He turned.

Gerald Sloan stood there, looking over Father Luke at Kline and then at the rest of the class. *Just exactly the wrong time for him to come. But I did say "anytime."* Father Wolfe smiled at the irony.

"No, Ger, this is just fine. Best time in the world. Do you want a seat? There's one right there behind

186

Desjardins." Father Wolfe had turned around to face Father Sloan and now gestured to the empty seat at the very back of the room. Father Sloan gingerly made his way past laughing students to the back row under the *Last Judgment* poster. *Well, that settles it. This is the end of the Luke Wolfe Teaching Road. God really has a sense of humor to inspire Sloan to visit this classic chaos—of all classes!*

"The Mouse-trap. Marry, how? This play is the image of a murder done in Vienna—" Larry-Hamlet was at his sardonic best. Even his thin-lipped half-smile only served to emphasize that he had total control of the situation.

Tiny, elfish Troy Wintergreen had cocooned himself in an orange poncho big enough for someone twice his size. Now, knees slowly jackknifing, he sidled toward the prostrate player king—who was making it clear that he was asleep by his stertorous and scene-stealing snoring from the other side of the front of the classroom—carrying a coffee cup.

"I forgot to tell you that Troy is the bad guy who wants the good king's crown and his good—well, on second thought she wasn't really that good—queen." Larry was saying this from his place at Ophelia's feet. "Those are *not*, by the way, exactly Shakespeare's lines. A little liberty here and there, you know." And he dismissed the comment with a backflip of his hand.

Troy knelt down beside the recumbent Greg Ferrell-Player King, coffee cup still in hand. But what was Troy doing? He set the coffee cup down on the floor and pulled out of his sleeve what looked like an enormous needle-ended syringe. It was the size of a caulking gun. Maybe it *was* a caulking gun. No, it was

187

a piece of cardboard stuck *over* a caulking gun with "POISON" in bold, neat blood-red letters. Tony brought the point up to Greg Farrell-Player King's carotid artery and held it as though trying to bring himself to effect the lethal deed.

"We thought we should kind of bring Shakespeare up to date, guys." This was Larry again. "What kind of poison is going to do any good poured into an ear? But a nice shot of air into an artery would do the damage. Besides, as Father pointed out in class, it's pretty hard to pour poison into *both* of a guy's ears—as Shakespeare had it—when he's sleeping on his side— as he has to if you're gonna pour it in at all."

"Why, you are better than a whole chorus." Al Flyte-Ophelia had fluted it just right—if not quite where Shakespeare had placed it. And now Al wore the satisfied smirk of the amateur comedian. And looked down. And blushed.

FIFTY-ONE

"Oh. Oh. Ohoh." It was half-gasped at Father Wolfe's ear. He tried to turn to see who it was. He could not turn. Someone was leaning against him. Whoever it was seemed catatonic. "Oh."

"You are soooo clever, Father. Too clever for your own good." All this in a whisper directly into and loud enough for only Father Wolfe's ear. Who was this? But the voice sounded very familiar. Father Wolfe found himself scratching his arm.

Troy had slipped the cardboard syringe up his wide sleeve again as he stood up. Greg Ferrell had stiffened two or three times in mock paroxysm and then collapsed in lifeless inertia.

Troy tiptoes away.

In delicately dances huge Player Queen-Harry Smathers and properly feigns surprise at her prostrate husband and frowns as a prelude to scolding him for sleeping so long. But then, after putting hand to his cheek, mocks her shock that he is dead.

"You knew all along, didn't you, Father?" It was the familiar voice behind him again.

Father managed to squirm around against the body beside him. It was Doctor Brandt. "Knew what, Doctor?"

"We were going to go for a little ride, just you and me so that no one else would ever find out what you discovered."

Just you and I, *Doctor. The subject of* were going.

"What did I discover?"

189

"And you had the kids put on this show to take me back to *Hamlet* and what Claudius has done and what I have done."

Oh, how I wish I had.

"I had no idea you were coming this morning, Doctor."

"Don't you check your voice-mail?" The whisper was sharp, angry, surprising from the gently smiling mouth.

Father Luke had. But there was nothing there when he had left at 7:20 for the classroom. And the classroom phone did not register voice mail.

"I phoned you at 7:37 and left the message that I would be here this morning precisely at 8:37. I guess that was a little too much for your Alzheimer's memory to handle."

"What *have* you done?"

"You know very well what I have done. You have known all along. That's why I tried to blindside you out of the play at the canal." That was a strange metaphor from such an obviously un-athletic man. "If you were killed or even ended up in the hospital, Greg could have gotten another teacher and saved his grade. Of course I killed my brother. You would have too. He was making such a mess of the whole business. Grandstanding and drawing attention to how much money we were making. Some people might have become upset enough to force us somehow to close the clinic. And now I am going to make it all. And Eudora will be mine—your play-acting notwithstanding." Anger little hindered this man's adroit dredging up of the archaic syntax. "But how did you know?"

"Why are you telling me all this, Doctor? Yes, I suspected that you might have been Dr. Curtland's killer—"

"And you were quite right. And you are going to die for all your meddling. Meddling with Peter Curtland. And my son. Now no one will know what you have discovered and used the students here to show me that you knew what I had done. This time it won't be a little nicotine. This time you are going to die right here in front of all these students of a heart attack."

It would have been more telling, Doctor, to have said, "This time, right in front of all these students, you are going to die of a heart attack."

You know how good I am at giving injections." And he smiled graciously and softly. The fluorescent light from the front of the room glanced off his glasses.

"But I have no flea bites, Doctor." He touched the fuzz on the top of his head.

"You figured that out too—the camouflage? But don't you think that was clever of me to take the opportunity of his having all those flea bites to mask the tiny red spot my hypodermic had entered to leave its delicate air bubble? How would the police ever know?"

"I guess they didn't."

"Lights. Lights." Kline-Claudius was shouting and stumbling past the darkened desks to the back of the classroom. Without thinking, Father Wolfe carelessly flipped the farther light switch.

And suddenly from behind the doctor came the stentorian and raucous "And where do you think you're going, young man?" of Jimmy Haley's talking frog. He had without thinking activated it with the gesture to turn the lights on.

"Who—?"

The class shouted in laughter at the apropos comment about the King's departure.

And before the doctor realized what had happened, with surprising agility for his 78 years, Father Wolfe had swung George LaPointe's Eight-Ball on top of Doctor Brandt's wrist. The syringe fell from his hand.

"I hope I'm not disturbing you two." Captain Parsons stood behind them at the open doorway of the classroom. He had a very black gun—small and squat, nothing like Clint Eastwood's big Colt—in his right hand. It was pointed at Doctor Brandt's head. With his left hand he removed a tiny earphone from his ear, attached to a thin cord that ran down to his chest pocket.

Father Wolfe laughed. "I think you are. And I'm glad. I don't know about the Doctor here. This is unexpected, Captain. What brings you here?"

"The Humvee, Father." Were the police driving those things now? "We kept questioning the two kids who bashed into you. And it didn't make any real sense."

Lieutenant Higgins had slipped around behind Doctor Brandt and was quietly and efficiently fastening the handcuffs, in spite of the Doctor's squirming. And threats of dire legal actions.

"Finally one of them became aware that they would have to take the whole punishment instead of the doctor here. And that didn't sit too well. They said that Doctor Brandt had put them up to it and had slipped out and left them to hold the bag on the promise of $1000 apiece if they would take the blame and say nothing about his having been there with them. So I wanted to talk to the Doctor. We went to his house and then to his clinic. His secretary there told us he had come over here to see Father Wolfe—something he apparently had been doing rather frequently of late.

"Why don't you come with me down to my office, now, Doctor? You can explain what that Humvee 'accident' was all about. And what you just said to Father Wolfe. I heard it all. And have it all right here." He patted his shirt pocket.

"But before we do that, let me read you your rights so that everything is kosher."

Well, that didn't sound very Eagle Scout-ish.

"What's going on here?" It was Father Sloan. And behind him in monotone Captain Parsons was intoning *Miranda*. He had come to the doorway from the back of the classroom. "Is these two gentlemen"—he nodded at the officer and the doctor—"all part of your class drama?"

Gerry never could get the number right on inverted sentences. "Umm. No." Was Gerry kidding? He couldn't really be serious. But then there was that literal streak in him.

FIFTY-TWO

"Well, did you like it, Father? Will we get the Snickers bars for the best play? Oh, excuse me. I didn't know you were talking to Father Sloan, Father."

"Not really, Ger." He turned to Larry. "It was very well done, Lar. But we still have to see the others."

"Father Wolfe, Father Wolfe." The bell had rung and Mrs. Smetana under full sail pushed her way through the students leaving the class.

"Yes, but they can't be as professional as ours was." Larry removed his yellow wig and laughed and was gone.

"I couldn't explain to Mrs. Lott where your classroom was."

Didn't you know that the Lott lady had been here just a couple of days ago?

Mrs. Smedana sounded as though she had just run the mile in less than four minutes. "So I left the switchboard and brought her over. I have to run. Father, Mrs. Lott wants to talk to you." She had managed to get next to the priest. And now she leaned over at him. Her voice was a hoarse whisper. "Don't let us down, Father. Don't let us down."

"I'll try not—"

"*Ms*. Lott." The tall lady was fast approaching from the port side.

"I'll be back later when the class puts on *Hamlet*, Father." Mrs. Smedana could not resist a shot over the bow. "My Harry said he was to play Horatio—a very important character, too, he says—in their play, but I have to run back to the switchboard now."

"Well, congratulations, Father Wolfe." Somehow they had moved into the hallway, and Ms. Lott was towering over him.

"Not today, Mrs. Smedana. Tomorrow perhaps." And Mrs. Smedana puffed off down the hall.

KNOT's Junior Miss-sized camerawoman was swimming against the ebb tide to get close enough for a clear shot. Students on the way out of the classroom were streaming past him from behind her back.

"This is Channel KNOT and your roving reporter Lyda Lott. We have here Father Luke who has solved the Peter Curtland murder which has mystified our police for the last week. You will remember that Doctor Curtland was the abortion provider whose son was accused of having killed him. And Father Wolfe here has unraveled this mystery. First, by pointing out it could not have been Peter Curtland's son Larry that killed him. And now by deducing the identity of the real murderer, by having his students enact the tragedy and, finally, by calling in the police to apprehend him. Are you glad you caught the murderer, Father?"

How could he explain to her that she had it all backwards? "Ms. Lott, I have nothing to say."

"I do." It was Father Sloan. "I am delighted to join you, Mrs. Knott—"

"Ms. Lott." The camera woman somehow managed the correction loud enough to be heard from behind the camera.

"—in congratulating Father Wolfe. I am sure his extraordinary mental acumen made this all possible." Father Sloan smiled as though he himself were being congratulated—had achieved the impossible. "And has brought recognition for just that sort of didactic to this

John Becker, S.J.

already renowned educational institution." He turned his warmest smile on Father Wolfe. "Thank you, Father Wolfe."

FIFTY-THREE

As if on cue, just as the television camera light snapped off, Mrs. Curtland was at Father Wolfe's side.

"I guess I'm a little late, Father." She shyly smiled her famished smile at him. "Larry told me he might be putting on their *Hamlet* play today, and Arthur"—yes, Arthur was standing behind her—"and I did want to see it. Especially since he seems to be himself again. Larry, that is. With your help. Thank you."

"Yes, that was the bell that ended the class. And, yes, Larry's group put on their—"

"Father, the TV people. The police." How had she missed them on her way in? "What are they doing here?"

"The police have arrested Doctor Brandt for the murder of your husband. And the TV people wanted it on the news tonight."

Eudora Curtland was obviously stunned. She blinked twice. "Oh." Was she going to faint? No, she slowly eased back into Arthur, who brought his arms up around his mother to support her. And with him she turned and headed for the front entrance of the building. Had she whispered "Oh, George" as she turned away from Father Luke?

FIFTY-FOUR

"Well, Father Wolfe, I must say you have really developed a dandy Dramatic Didactic that is definitely different from anything we have ever seen before."

Do you realize, Gerry, that you have developed alliteration-itis?

"It just doesn't parallel any of the pedagogical paradigms we are constantly being prodded to move toward by our more philosophically persuaded Jesuit brothers. And I do not remember my *Hamlet* very well—it has been a long time, Father"—he looked over and into Father Wolfe's eyes owlishly, as though this was a deep truth that needed pondering—"and I do not know how far they were going in taking liberties with Shakespeare."

Father Wolfe said nothing. What did all this mean? For his continued teaching? Or, for that matter, anything else?

They were walking from the school building to the dining room in the Jesuit residence for lunch. And Father Sloan was at his gracious best. "But I must admit that since KLOT—was that the name of the channel?—was here with that enormous woman reporter and your name and face will be all over the TV screen and in all the papers, I might just have to eat some humble pie."

"Sarah told me this morning she was going to boil up a huge pot of her famous hot dogs." *Why, dammit, do I always have to be flip with Gerry?* He looked over and up into Gerry Sloan's eyes. How was he taking this?

"And what with your Dynamic Didactic so deftly demonstrated—" Father Sloan with his left hand pushed his glasses up over his forehead and rubbed both eyes with the same hand. "This will take a bit of thinking." They had almost reached the door to the lunch room.

Father Wolfe suddenly realized he had been taking small steps. He stretched out into his buck private mile-eating gait, swallowed the pain and then noted that it disappeared.

"But later. What was it you said? Hot dogs? I hope she has some of her onion-heavy potato salad."

FIFTY-FIVE

"Father Wolfe." Captain Parsons' authoritative voice caught him just before he swung through the door behind Gerry Sloan. "I have a confession to make."

"A confession?"

"But first, thank you for all of your cooperation in this whole Peter Curtland business. We never could have broken the case without you.

"I have to admit to you, though"—he dropped his eyes from Father Wolfe's face to the priest's shirtfront—"that we knew—well, we were pretty close to certain—from almost the very beginning that the murderer of Doctor Curtland was Doctor Brandt." He brushed his mustache as though it were developing an independent mind of its own. "Forensics immediately found a bubble of air right at the heart. And that was explained by none of the candidates' possible attempts except Doctor Brandt's needle. So we had to—umm—embroider the truth a little for you."

"And so I was your guinea pig."

"Well, that's a little harsh, Father." He smiled a little boy I'm-sorry-Mom smile. "But we did hope that the good—or not so good—Doctor would show his hand. Although the kids and the Humvee business"—the Captain looked off into the parking lot, obviously embarrassed—"put the lid on any hesitance we had about his guilt, we still needed a confession of some kind to make the accusation stick. And you set him up for just that." Captain Parsons was again looking at Father Luke with a smile that asked forgiveness.

"Captain, I had no idea—"

"Yes, Father, that's fine." Captain Parsons was still smiling as he looked Father Wolfe directly in the eyes. "But take the credit where the credit is due."

"But—"

"Thank you." And he slipped into his Ford patrol car, waved and was gone.

God bless you, Captain.

FIFTY-SIX

Chollie,

Well, the Peter Curtland Murder is no longer a mystery. It's a fait accompli.

Except for the trial and all and whatever happens to poor Doctor Brandt.

I should have known from the beginning that he was the "perp" as Captain Parsons has taught me to say. But somehow I never made the connection that the Doctor himself immediately made. The one that was pounding on my door and I was deaf to. A perfect parallel to Claudius and Gertrude and Hamlet.

And David and Bathsheba. And John Finney's candid assessment of what was going on. And had the lady protested too much? And. And.

Why didn't I see through it all with these promptings?

And what would Captain Parsons have done if he had not as good as confessed in open court?

I only wish that Gerry had been concrete and affirmative. Did that "humble pie" have another year here for me in the recipe?

Guess you gotta keep leaning on the Holy Spirit if I am to continue doing the one thing I love with a passion. Yes, yes, I know, I know, I know that I am committed to what God tells me to do through my Superiors. And—gulp!—I will. Anything less seems so completely

*unworthy of my due return to Jesus. But, still,
see what you can do for me. OK?*

Luke

FIFTY-SEVEN

"Hiya, Father Luke. Correct my paper yet?" Lighthearted. Buoyant. Slightly mocking.

It was early Monday evening. A jubilant mockingbird outside the window was telling the world that he was happy and the whole world should be too. Father Luke had come over to his classroom to try to correct a few papers. And maybe even collect his thoughts.

"Just thought we'd stop by." It was Tony Santos, of course, with his arm around the waist of a diminutive girl with a Barbie-Doll perfect face and a Barbra Steisand nose who went by the name of Rita Poulos.

She wriggled just a little against him and smiled at Fr. Luke. It was a knowing smile. They possessed a secret.

"No, I haven't, Ton." He smiled at them. "And at the rate I'm going, I won't get many papers done tonight. Just too much running through this old head."

"We just stopped by." Tony obviously had something on his mind. "And hoped you would be here and the building would be open. We didn't want to disturb you over at the Jesuit house." They were standing in front of his desk now.

"You have probably worried that we'd—umm—let our relationship become—umm—too intimate."

Father Wolfe looked straight at him over his reading glasses, then took them off and gently placed them on the desk in front of him.

"Every once in a while you say something in class about how important it is to really love other human beings. Especially those you think you love. Not just what they can give you. And certainly not just pleasure. Because the pleasure in God's plan is for a purpose."

Father Wolfe sat staring at Tony. Fascinated. A student had actually paid attention to what he said.

"And since we love each other so much, we have decided to do just that—to love one another and not just for the pleasure of—umm—intimacy." Why didn't he say "sex"? He knew the priest knew the word.

"And since Tony and I"—Rita had picked up her part in the dialogue, as she toyed with the green pen on Father Wolfe's desk—"knew just how difficult it would be—so many other kids are so casual about God's gift to give life—to make sure we'll do it God's way, we have promised one another that we will go to Mass every morning together. Our best way to pray for God's power in our love and to thank Him for it." Rita smiled up from her eyelashes. Another secret she and Tony and the priest shared. "The seven-thirty at St. Ignatius next door. Just before school."

It was Father Luke's turn to smile. "I love it, you–"

"Oof. Father." Tony was suddenly anxious. "I almost forgot. I promised my brother I'd have the Jeep back by eight. And—see you tomorrow, Father."

They half-ran, half-danced to the door, stopped momentarily for a quick wave and a smile. And were gone.

Well, Lord, as somebody said, if You didn't create woman to make sure men could find You, You sure have been doing a great job of fooling us all.

Father Luke settled back in his chair. The mockingbird in the jacaranda was certainly happy about something. For an instant Janey was right there in the classroom. Laughing.

Good hunting, Jesus.